Elusive Plato

Rhys Hughes

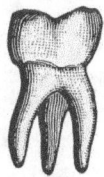

Bizarro Pulp Press
an imprint of JournalStone Publishing

This is a work of fiction. All of the characters, names, incidents, organizations, and dialogue in this novel are either the products of the author's imagination or are used fictitiously.

Bizarro Pulp Press books may be ordered through booksellers or by contacting:

Bizarro Pulp Press, a JournalStone imprint
    www.BizarroPulpPress.com

    ISBN: 978-1-945373-01-5

Printed in the United States of America
JournalStone rev. date: April 30, 2016

    Cover Art: Matthew Revert

    Interior Formatting: Lori Michelle
        www.theauthorsalley.com

Praise for Rhys Hughes

"Rhys Hughes seems almost the sum of our planet's literature . . . As well as being drunk on language and wild imagery, he is also sober on the essentials of thought. He has something of Mervyn Peake's glorious invention, something of John Cowper Powys's contemplative, almost disdainful existentialism, a sensuality, a relish, an addiction to the delicious. He's as tricky as his own characters . . . He toys with convention. He makes the metaphysical political, the personal incredible and the comic hints at subtle pain. Few living fictioneers approach this chef's sardonic confections, certainly not in English."

—MICHAEL MOORCOCK

"Quirky and fantastic and sometimes quite twisted, Rhys Hughes is a treat for those in the mood for something utterly different."

—ELLEN DATLOW

"Rhys Hughes is an accomplished player with words, plots, effects, relationships, sensibilities; you name it, Hughes tries to stand it on its head. More often than seems attributable to mere chance, he succeeds."

—ED BRYANT, LOCUS

"Dazzling prose. Put your feet up and dip in. Life will never seem quite the same again."

—THE THIRD ALTERNATIVE

"I wore throughout the undisplaceable, unsequelchable rictus of a grin of both delight and amazement."

—MICHAEL BISHOP

"The incredible richness of language, the inexhaustible array of puns, double entendres, weird metaphors, non-lexical use of words, and original turns of phrase . . . Rhys Hughes is essentially an absurdist humorist, though often of a peculiarly black, tricky, and sometimes bloody sort. Much of his work is travesty, drawing for substance on other works, which he uses as a basis for destructive humor, for reinterpretation in a different mode, or as a starting point for his own work. This statement is not meant in disparagement, for Hughes's new versions are highly original in conception and often brilliant."

—SUPERNATURAL FICTION WRITERS (SCRIBNERS)

"Rhys Hughes is one of the most wildly inventive talents we are graced with today."

—ALL HALLOWS

"Hughes' world is a magical one, and his language is the most magical thing of all."

—T.E.D. KLEIN

"There are no easy phrases to describe Hughes' fiction; it's so exotic. His writing is incredibly precise and at the same time his imagination is so unfettered."

—JEFFREY FORD

"Hughes' similarity to Spike Milligan runs deeper than the occasional shared lurch of phrase, for he writes as though he'd been bloodied in the same wars Milligan fought for eight decades: the same up-yours melancholia about the malice of the absurd—about the absurdness of the world defined not only as an inherent lack of species-friendly grammar in the convulsion of the real, but also a sense that anyone who acts as though he believes what he is told by our Masters will almost necessarily inflict pain on others."

—JOHN CLUTE

"What do I like about Rhys Hughes's work? Fun. Hughes sees and precipitates in words the latent humour in almost anything. Ranging from what our culture considers pleasing and smilingly ridiculous to horrors that have to be laughed at if they are faceable at all, Hughes is a laughing observer, both inside and outside. With Hughes you get humour that is white, various shades of grey, black—

and I don't know why humour cannot be characterized by other colours. I am also enormously impressed by Hughes's stylistic brilliance. The richness of language, the occasional Cambrianisms, the inexhaustible array of puns, weird metaphors that form the point of a story. And I envy him his netted imagination. As a man who sees connections where others do not, he offers enough ideas, if parcelled out, to fill a catalogue of fantasy for a generation of writers."

—E.F. BLEILER

"It's a crime that Rhys Hughes is not as widely known as Italo Calvino and other writers of that stature. Brilliantly written and conceived, Hughes' fiction has few parallels anywhere in the world. In some alternate universe with a better sense of justice, his work triumphantly parades across all bestseller lists. "

—JEFF VANDERMEER

"If Hughes ever stops writing fiction I will shoot him."

—JEFF VANDERMEER

"Every Hughes story implies much, served with wit and whimsy and word-relish, high spirits and bittersweet twists."

—IAN WATSON

"A dazzling disintegration of the reality principle. A rite of passage to the greater world beyond common sense. Raises the bar on profundity and sets a comic standard for the tragic limits of our human experience. Like Beckett on nitrous oxide. Like Kafka with a brighter sense of humor."

—A.A. ATTANASIO

This book is
dedicated to
Brenda Skogmann

The house, with its dripping eaves and crumbling walls, the owl-haunted trees which strangled it, resembled a prehistoric growth that had refused to fossilise. A spirit of violent serenity suffused the chill rooms. My parents passed through the gloomy passages like perfumed shadows.

I grew up, for the most part, on the roof, among the noose of branches; and as these tightened, the highest chimney seemed to stiffen like the erection of a hanged man. When pale sparks spluttered from the flue—my mother baking bread no darker than a scared albino—the total effect was as sordid as the death agony of a tortured tramp.

I was weaned on the memories of a diseased past. Immediately after my birth, my mother poisoned the midwife by daring her to devour the steaming placenta. I was then baptised in sour wine and named in honour of a lunatic ancestor—Bartleby Cadiz. My earliest fantasies involved the kidnapping of village women who strayed into our domain.

But the notion of violating them with the body I possessed was abhorrent. I ached to alter my form, to mould it to a more suitable shape. As if caressing a metaphor for the shearing of my identity, my hands were fond of knives and they delighted in the weight and balance of a sharpened blade.

Few words were exchanged among our family. I taught myself to read, sneaking into my father's study at night to fondle the manuscripts. My callow efforts resulted in a speech without meaning but with a sibilant beauty that shattered the glassy eyes of my companion owls.

I realised I was struggling to tease language from a collection of musical scores. Father was a failed composer, the owner of an antique Bösendorfer piano. He turned the instrument insane with his unlikely chord sequences and jaded arpeggios. In lieu of a metronome, suspended over the keyboard on a hook, a rotting hunk of meat dropped maggots, the click of each grub on the dirty ivory marking time. The meat was his left foot, severed by an unknown creature in the flooded cellar.

I was not unhappy with my childhood, except at mealtimes. My mother thought it amusing to serve the most depressing fare available. Gathered around the lopsided table, my father and I would tremble as she offered us bowls of tinned peaches, with a thin cream floating on the juice like a slick.

On Sundays, in the gathering dusk, we listened to hymns on the short-wave radio in an attempt to anticipate the sentiments. The dishes were licked clean by one of our nameless cats and father would rest his stump on my back as I made obeisance to the bland divinity.

"A footstool carved from a single child!" he would joke, while mother opened her box of leeches and clamped them over her sores.

There was an unhealthy portion of anguish in all his humour. On one occasion, after being served a double helping, he threw down his napkin and stood up. We watched him stalk off with hooded eyes. The inevitable came within a minute: a minor chord vibrating through the corridors like a spider's web struck with a tuning fork. We stepped out of the kitchen and caught him dangling in the stairwell. Three piano wires were looped around his throat, sounding the weight of his despair.

This auto-elegy was as unsatisfying as all his music. It lingered in the house from that evening, settling in recesses like an atonal mist. I was unsure of the point of his gesture, its wasted poignancy, but mother was delighted and called for a blue-glass bottle.

I ran to fetch one and returned to find her loosening his belt. He still kicked and writhed, for the fall had not broken his neck. She did not bother to pull down his trousers—his own thrashings soon accomplished this. Father, who considered underwear a sign of dementia, looked absurd in the sinful flesh. As I giggled, his warty member uncurled and speared toward me like the accusing finger of an offended ogre.

2

Elusive Plato

I gagged on the stench and buried my face in my sleeve, at the same time tasting a rare delicacy in the morbid flavour. Meeting his horrid gaze, mother stepped forward and touched the instrument of copulation. It jumped in her hand and she deftly caught the spurting seed, filling the tiny bottle to the brim and corking it with her earwax.

We buried him in the garden, using the scatological excesses which he also loosed to fertilise the soil. We planted petunias and marigolds over his grave, the only flowers we knew by name. We avoided his study, the cluttered adjuncts of his being: the empty notebooks, jars of green ink, the diving suit nailed to a wall like a messiah.

Mother retired to her room with the bottle, where she conducted unusual experiments with the viscous liquid—she was a student of eugenics and alchemy. After a period of fruitless research, she drafted a letter to a renowned occult savant in London, requesting advice. Her motives were pure: she wanted to recreate father in a superior idiom.

In the hall, a stunted grandfather clock bristling with weird dials helped her calculate the positions of sundry planets. Astrological maps covered every table. I often saw her silhouetted on the curtains of the highest oriel, hands between her legs. While capering on the roof, I heard her whimper below, neither in pain nor pleasure but with an objectivity that was shocking.

I noticed her swelling stomach before she announced the pregnancy. Father had been impotent since my dramatic conception, and so his posthumous virility was an engaging irony.

"The first time he has been faithful to me," she confessed.

Despite her growing bulk, she managed to tread the bare floorboards soundlessly. When it became obvious the pregnancy was not a phantom, she used the last of the seed in a pearly joke. One Sabbath, the cream on my sallow fruit swirled more alive than ever.

The jest was a failure; I had been warned. Mystic runes had been cut into the bannister by father's wires and these formed my oracle. My nonchalance alarmed her. I obliged by vomiting into a napkin. The runes also suggested she would invite me to share her moist bed, but her condition had attenuated her lust. I stole thrills by dangling from the eaves and watching her undress. Eventually, she allowed me to place my ear to her turgid abdomen, to listen for an extra heart. Instead, I detected a sigh.

I assisted at the birth, cutting the umbilical cord with a pair of blunt scissors. The child was a girl, remaining as nameless as our other animals. We shut her in the attic until she became a useful slave.

After this lacuna, my life improved: I taught her to converse in Latin, lifted her onto the slates and showed her how to leap from chimney to tree over dizzying heights. I fed her insects and worms by the handful. In quieter moments, I stuck her with pins until she resembled an anthropomorphic cactus. She took my slights with ignorant grace, smiling as I forced the needles under her smooth skin. Mother, who kept father's studded belt to lash her with, deemed my torments amateurish.

I rigidly believed I would taste the fruits of her sexuality almost as soon as she matured. Desperate to lose my virginity, I thought myself not unlovely, though somewhat skeletal. Accordingly, scarcely a day went by without me removing her clothing to judge her ripeness. The instant a single hair coiled from her pudenda, I knew I would pounce. I thought it poor taste to break into her prepubescent body, an impatient exploiter.

While we waited, to pass the time melodically, I explained the complete theory of music. She was a fast learner, improvising songs and monstrous madrigals that racked me with convulsions.

One afternoon, mother sent me into the village on a trivial errand. She claimed that she wanted to purchase a timepiece for her bedroom. In the cold drizzle, the streets of Horam were empty. I passed the row of curio shops, peering through each window.

With a pocketful of change, I found the local brothel unavoidable. I rang the doorbell and was admitted by a sardonic housewife in a leather skirt. She counted my money, insisted I only had enough for a basic service and led me to a small chamber hung with red draperies.

She undressed with disconcerting speed and beckoned for me to follow her example. I hastened to divest myself of trousers and shirt, while she wound an alarm clock by the bed.

When I glanced up, she was nude, drumming her fingers on her thigh. At once my desire became curiously hollow. Her breasts, firm and shiny, reminded me of the throats of toads. I was sorry not to see them pulsate in time with her breathing. Her nipples, large as noses, were unsuitable for my dainty mouth. But it was the mass of hair between her legs, where my sister had an unhealed wound, that made me cancel the transaction.

It was the familiar reluctance of my fantasies. Although I appreciated the quality of her curls, I did not wish to pass through them as a man. Inspecting her mahogany spirals, it seemed to me that such silky exuberance required a more lateral approach.

The housewife accepted my change of heart without question, but I was unable to secure a refund. I made sure she preceded me out of the chamber and I deftly pocketed the alarm clock. Slinking out into the rain, I reflected on my unexplained needs. The woman had interested me, but I could not express my passion with my present carnal topography.

Changes in my physical structure were urgently required. What was the nature of such alterations? Without this insight, I would not be able to adjust the erotic iconography of my subconscious. I loped through the woods, reaching the house before the fully-wound clock in my pocket ignited. The building lay shuddering like a nauseated uncle.

In the musty atmosphere of the hall, I paused to listen. Above me, as if from a moulting angel, feathers were drifting in the still air. A gasp of unseen ecstasy turned the many corners of the unwieldy staircase and disturbed these downy tokens. I stood on tiptoe and snatched one in my cruel fist. The odour of penetration coated it like salt.

I bounded up the steps, five at a time, and reached my mother's bedroom. The door was ajar. As I pushed it fully open, three concurrent events of a minor but grisly tone sewed me into disappointment's flaccid stomach. I fell to my knees and lapped my own tears.

My mother had beaten me to possession of my sister. In my absence, the young girl had blossomed like a ghost-orchid. A single hair, as long as a dwarf's whip, undulated in the air directly above her clitoris. Her head was at an unnatural angle, little teeth rending a pillow.

My mother had not hesitated—wedged between my sister's narrow thighs, her tongue curled like a bracket around the aching bud. I recognised in this vista a parallel with ancient lore. The inhabitants of Lesbos, an island, had once practised such caresses. Curious race memories stirred in my blood. This was the first affecting truth.

I turned from it to a regard of the second. In the triptych of cold mirrors on the dressing table, each prism angled inwards, I confronted a reflection of my kneeling self imposed over the entwined couple.

As my sister thrust upward, it seemed I shared the sweet effluvia that dripped from the perimeter of her vulva. As I gargled on the illusion, the alarm clock exploded against my suddenly hateful manhood. This last revelation was the most powerful, loosening my enamelled preconceptions like eroded teeth in rotting gums—a final recall to my masculinity. When the clock exhausted itself, I continued its screech.

My mother looked up from her prone position, mouth wet with pungent sap. I lunged forward and pulled her hair, dragging her from her meal. As we tussled, my sister rolled free and fled. I chewed mother's tongue, indirectly tasting the young wine of my undefined sibling. My blows had some of the quality of joyous caresses. I knew at last the purpose of my jealousy. Slapping the daggers of her thumbs away from my throat, I let loose the startling revelation.

I cried: "I want to be a sapphist as well!"

At this, mother fell back, her putrefying laughter washing me in a miasma of indescribable foulness.

"That is a somewhat unrealistic ambition."

I was determined not to listen to logic. Sweeping out of the room, I climbed through the landing window and gained the roof. Here, I mulled over my astounding insight. I was a lesbian trapped inside a man's body! With this knowledge came ambiguous relief.

I had come out of a closet resembling an iron maiden, only to find myself confronting other dungeon tortures. How could I ever express my male tribadism? The plateau of my sexuality was unattainable. No metaphysical thumbscrew, however well it pulped reality's digit, could change this simple fact. So my reason was unseated; I foamed at mouth and eyes. Steaming in the rain, I twisted my loathsome flap, my knotted root.

How long I sat there can be judged from the level to which I ground my teeth. Before that event, my molars were like headstones, crooked but exquisitely marbled. After, they resembled paved avenues leading towards a single sepulchre.

Elusive Plato

I was roused from my perch by a sound I thought had been denied to the world's sanity. Father's piano was rumbling from the deeps of his study. I crawled on the ivy until I reached his window and glanced in. My sister, still unclothed, was carefully reconstructing his lost chords. Seated on the low stool, her pubic hair waved in rhythm to the horrid melodies. I was confronting an inverted gorgon, the result of the union of living and dead: a freak.

I returned to the landing, swinging myself through the casement and falling into my mother's arms. Aghast, she crossed herself fervently and I slipped from her embrace.

"What are we to do?" she whispered.

She was in the last throes of a religious desperation. I was unable to proffer an adequate reply. Amplified by the corridors, the music had taken on a lugubrious quality, each congealing note trapped in the bars like petty thieves in a gibbet. I suggested we adopt the child as an honorary father. If a patriarch was peeled, would not the core be indistinguishable from my cursed sister? My mother was unimpressed.

"Then we must kill her as we would any father," I said. "Brush her with olive oil and roast her."

"She is already dead to me. It is burial she lacks."

It was not the audible music which disturbed us, but what remained unplayed. The wires that had strangled father, and had ultimately been responsible for my sibling's existence, had never been replaced. As my sister ranged the length of the stained keyboard, the three notes forming the niggling chord were deafening in their absence.

This occult frequency impaled us on fangs of remorse. Feathers from the torn pillow, not yet settled, froze in the solid air. In panic, we descended to the security of the living room. Nameless cats, tails erect, prickled like maces. In the hearth, coals tumbled melodramatically.

"We might dress her in his clothes and break her on a wheel of his bicycle. Like a peripatetic martyr."

"That, Bartleby, is facetious."

Huddling under the table, mother conjured a scheme in the dust. As my hands were so clever with knives, I should use a blade to lever her out of the study. Like a putrefying oyster, we must seek to swallow her whole. A grave would accomplish this; a fitting maw to chew the dead.

I could secure her limbs, carry her out into the garden, cast her over the edge of a freshly dug pit. The Bösendorfer, minus internal organs, would make a perfect coffin. Shedding basilisk tears, we might intone an elegy as absent as father's penumbral opus. And his jars of ink, stacked like emerald skulls, would form the headstone.

Reaching out, mother pulled the tablecloth free, scattering plates like petrified tongues. She pushed it into my arms. "The winding sheet," she announced. I held the soiled bundle close; the odour of peach juice, spilled in days of fretful innocence, was unbearable. "Wrap her tight," she continued, "and keep the horror tranquil."

I emerged from our sanctuary, collected my favourite knife from the pantry, and climbed the stairs. I also picked up another cherished item, one kept secret from my mother. Outside the study, the nonexistent chord strung out my bones like washed linen. I flapped in the excess; with a mighty howl, I leaped into the swirling room. The scene resembled the retelling of an opium dream; a ghastliness as oblique as a guillotine. I dipped my poniard into my regurgitated enigma.

My father's possessions, shards of his being, chattered in time to his modal resurrection. The mouldering notebooks rustled, the metronome rotted backwards, the diving suit jerked like a deflated epileptic. The piano seemed an unattainable distance away.

I struggled forward, ears burning with the silent cacophony. When I reached my sister, I began to pinch her thighs. They slowly parted and I eased my poisoned steel into her undeveloped womb. It met little resistance. Her fingers curled back from the keyboard; I moved the knife in a circular motion, a gesture of affection. She found a harrowing scream in her repertoire. I pushed the hilt upwards, angling my shoulder under the handle. With the tearing of birth, I prised her off the stool.

Quick as a centipede, I tangled her in the folds of the tablecloth. She did not struggle, but my father's breath poured from her lungs. Icy and foolish, it formed patterns of frost on my chin. I finished bundling her, slotted her into the spare shelf of a bookcase and summoned mother.

She came up with a saw and we eviscerated the piano. Without a frame, it was light enough to bounce down the stairs into the garden. Assuming my sister was safely restrained, we dug a hole with the nervous energy of frightened vampires; when it was ready, we lowered the shell and leaned on our shovels to express relief.

It was only a temporary respite. Looking up, mother let out a yell and plucked at my sleeve. At the study window, my sister peered down at us with an expression of undiluted astonishment. She had managed to partly wriggle out of her winding sheet: a grub in the wrong chrysalis.

With tender fingers, she traced an indistinct symbol in the condensation on the glass. I made out five parallel lines and three winking circles. Then the rain ceased and a fissure, as narrow as sewn labia, gaped in the monochrome clouds. A ray of dying sun struck the casement. The dripping sigil was revealed as notes on a stave—the forbidden chord!

Mother was frantic. "We must finish the funeral before suppertime. Hurry inside and fetch her."

"I will not," I replied. "I left my knife in her vagina. Without it I cannot imagine a confrontation."

"Do this for me, Bartleby, and you shall have an early inheritance. Enough even for your morbid tastes."

This promise, one denied to most mortals, thrilled me into violent action. I rushed into the house and spiralled up to the study. My sister stumbled out and evaded my grasp; I chased her through the corridors. It was unlikely my words could persuade her to yield.

She vanished into the bathroom and hid among the leaking pipes and hastily repaired spiders. A smugness I did not feel directed my steps. Crooning, I edged into damp shadows, tiles slippery with antique smears of despicable soap, carvings of human fat. Obese droplets chimed.

In the intestinal tangle of lead piping, she cowered starkly. There was much of the divine about her: her grubby whiteness was the colour of bishop semen, her jaw chattered like a cat that has feasted on a crippled angel. Skirting the iron bath, with its hidden generator and electrodes, I approached like a malevolent masseur.

She jumped up with a sickly laugh and scrabbled at the skylight. I snatched the end of the tablecloth, but it tore in my hand as she broke the glass and climbed onto the tiles. I was obliged to follow. Back in my elemental realm, my confidence knew no bounds. I stalked her over the gabled heights, weaving into the forest of warped chimneys—some used, many merely decorative, most leading to rooms we had never discovered.

Because I had taught her well, her balance could not be compromised by taunts. I hurled insults, imprecations, promises as false as the walls of the house—but all to no avail. She refused to be dislodged by sentences, despite the poetry of their hatred, the grammatically perfect flow of their irregular and debauched verbs.

The furthest wing of the house, dilapidated and malodorous, reared over the garden like a cancerous monkey. Here, at the limits of my old world, she turned to face me. The forgiveness in her eyes made me want to retch with humility; I envied the martyrdom she was claiming.

Below, mother shook her fist. I guessed her alarm: my sister had to be buried alive, as a modulus to father's funeral, if we were to finally snap the conductor's baton of his phantasmagorical silence. Like a minor opera, the finale had to be extreme but unmemorable. Playing the suicide card, like a gambler who keeps an emotion up a sleeve, she was going to cheat us with a plummeting ovation.

She tottered there, a frail apparition, long enough for me to feel sympathy. Then she threw herself off. But there is some justice in this world after all: as she fell, the wind filled her winding sheet like a parachute and lowered her gently into the grave. Mother squeaked as the bundle settled into the piano; she slammed the lid shut with her foot and shovelled dirt in a frenzy of redemption.

I descended from the roof—the long way—and assisted her in the mouldy task. We patted the earth down firmly, erected the headstone and stood back to admire our work. The two graves, father's parallel to my sister's, were like faceless tarot cards from a forgotten pack. All the things I saw there—wealth, success, insouciance—were an echo of imminent reward, my premature inheritance.

I reminded mother of her promise. She scowled and sought to change the subject. I was stubborn and she finally acquiesced. We entered the house and she led me to the basement steps.

"It is down there—every single penny. On the floor of the flooded cellar. In a heavy sunken chest."

"But why hide it in such an inaccessible place?"

"The cellar once was dry. It lies directly below the bathroom. The leaking pipes have slowly filled the vault with foul water. We acted too late. Now recovery is hazardous."

"The unknown creature . . . "

"The thing that took my husband's foot off was our first child. It always thwarted his attempts at diving for the treasure. In jest, as you know, I substituted semen for cream on your peaches. Years ago, I played the opposite joke on your father. When he finally managed to impregnate me, it was with ideal milk."

I grimaced. "An abortion?"

"The foetus did not develop properly; I miscarried into the cellar. It did not die. It adapted to the environment—flippers and fins. Half its nature is that of substitute cream: an instinct to swim. Also, when carrying, I was frightened by a fish . . . "

"What can I do to evade it?"

"That is your problem. I will watch but not help. When your father dived, I worked a winch to haul him to the surface. All in vain. The beast guards the treasure jealously."

This was truly exasperating. Railing against mother for her trick, I fell to pondering a solution. I reasoned that the main difficulty lay not in diving down but in coming back up. How would I manage this on my own? I examined the cellar carefully. Above the stinking pool, a pulley had been bolted to the ceiling. At once, the answer was obvious. But I needed to clarify some details.

I turned to face mother. Oblivious of my presence, she squatted and started milking a breast into the hungry lake—a pasteurised ritual. When she had finished, I asked:

"Do housewives float?"

She frowned at the question. But her devotion to science outweighed her suspicion of my motives.

"Most do not. Like engineers and lyricists, they contain almost no air. The ancient authors are agreed. Among the moderns, only Papus Levi disputes this. He claims to have witnessed one drifting down the Thames. I laid a housewife once, but not in water."

That night, after refusing to join her for supper, I retired to my favourite gable and prayed for success. The clouds had melted. Through the trees, the lights of the village twinkled hypocritically. As soon as she was safely in bed, I crept down and searched the study for plans of the building, finding some in a locked bureau. They were clearly marked with the cellar's depth.

Also, I spent an hour leafing through father's diaries, reading accounts of his numerous failed dives. The creature was ostensibly male and had taken up residence in the treasure chest itself. It emerged whenever he touched down on the floor of the flooded chamber but not before. On his final dive, mother had been too slow in winching him up and it had caught him.

In the cupboard under the stairs, I glided my sensitive hands over coils of rope. In her bedroom, where my sister's scent waned as she suffocated in her aesthetic tomb, mother snored in mixolydian mode. She clutched a stuffed bear. Her body contours were those of a pestilential swamp, no reliable paths between the notable features. The alarm clock protruded from her sex, as if she sought to conjoin with time. I fumed at this setback; I needed the device to implement my scheme. Unmovable, smothered by her yodelling yoni, it acted the part of a prolapsed womb, groped by mutilated and slow-moving hands.

It was necessary to arrange an alternative. In the hall, I lifted the stunted grandfather clock onto my back. I carried it carefully into the woods and toward the village. Horam was dozing; I knocked on the door of the brothel and the prostitute, dishevelled at the end of her shift, answered with a yawn. Her auburn brows knitted as she beheld my faded silks and anaemic stubble.

"What do you want? You stole my clock."

"Consumed with guilt, I have come to offer a replacement." I rested the grandfather on the threshold.

"That's a very small one," she said. She examined it with a measure of disdain. "This clock is crippled."

I bowed. "My grandfather lost his legs in Auschwitz."

She clapped a tiny hand to her full mouth. "Oh, I am sorry. It must have been terrible for him . . . "

"Yes, he fell from a watchtower."

The present mollified her and I was able to arrange another session of sexual congress. She took my hand to lead me inwards, but I shook my head. She stared at me in bewilderment.

"I am unable to perform in these surroundings. The red draperies do not titillate. You must come to my house."

"That will cost at least double. How can I be sure you'll pay? You have cheated me once already . . . "

"I have been saving my pocket money for many weeks. You may judge the weight of my piggy bank for yourself."

After a little more banter, I persuaded her to follow me. Her tight skirt was not conducive to walking. She tripped in my wake, the sort of woman who is distrustful of trees. It was as if my first fantasies were coming true, a ripe beauty entering my kingdom, ready to be peeled.

As I studied her at frequent intervals, I found it impossible to recall what she looked like under her clothes. It was a technique she had perfected to maintain a regular clientele. I envied her body, the nipples hard as limes, the roll of her married hips. I found her tarnished domesticity thrilling. The moonlighting housewife is still my type. Women who can cook badly are utterly bewitching.

She was astounded by the existence of the house, an edifice she had been warned about as a child but had never accepted as real. Scepticism continues to protect us from agents of the government. Once indoors, I had to move quickly. Mother would chide me for bringing a harlot home. All had to be accomplished before she awoke. I ordered the floozy to undress in the hall while I flustered up the stairs.

"I shall be back in a moment. Feel free to admire the furniture." I did not wait to hear her response.

I struggled into the necessary costume and descended with arthritic motions. She gasped at my appearance, my warped visage through the thick glass of the helmet. Tubes coiled like innards. Quickly, she resumed her professional stance, hand on hip, reflex smirk.

"Kinky tastes? I've had all sorts."

"Help me with the oxygen cylinders," I pleaded, my voice muffled. I was feeling faint with the exertion.

She had stripped only to her stockings. She took hold of the tanks and strapped them to my back. The diving suit was father's invention; he once explained its workings to me, while I made notes. Inside, the heat was stifling; I felt like the liver of a desiccated whale. My gauntleted hand beckoned at the door.

"Through here. This is where I want you."

She ventured into darkness. Steps jerked down to the liquid. The rope was already in position, threaded through the pulley, cut to the exact length. I instructed her to tie one end to the hook on my head, then I asked her to attach herself to the other. To my amazement, she allowed me to loop it under her shoulders. I tied a clumsy knot, the best I was able to do, a desperate gamble. If it did not hold, my marvellous life would very shortly be over.

"Now jump in," I said, "and meet my brother."

Suddenly, the ludicrous horror of her situation assailed her. She sought to retreat. I pushed her and she tumbled through space, landing on her back. Her expression was lost in the gloom of the unlit cellar. She called out a colloquial curse. Then she vanished into the abyss. When the rope pulled taut, I knew she had reached the bottom. It was a question of exact timing. I lowered myself after her. The chill winded me; I sank like a poetical technician.

Beneath the opaque surface, the waters were illuminated by a green radiance. The luminous walls poured an eldritch glow into the chamber. I could plainly discern the furnishings of the cell: the wine racks, full of outdated Amontillado, the broken ladders and senile adding machines. Also, bones of plucked architects, original designers of our unpraised folly.

Heavier than the whore, I acted like a counterweight, pulling her back to the surface. Soon we passed each other, the halfway point, and I grimaced in sardonic greeting.

There was something pursuing her. I had judged everything to utter perfection. She had struck bottom and roused the creature, my brother, from his lair, leaving the treasure chest unguarded. At this point, her ascent was rapid enough to preserve her from his jaws. Encased in iron, I made a less attractive meal; he did not even glance at me as our paths crossed. His bloated sperm-like form was not particularly repulsive, but the undulations of his body were uniquely vile.

I touched the floor and struggled to maintain my balance. I had but a few seconds to accomplish my plan. I had stopped falling, so the whore had stopped rising—my brother would catch her. He would surely want to drag her to his abode; I was relying on this.

I embraced the chest not a moment too soon: the rope jerked and I was pulled up at a velocity that numbed my brain. Again, I passed the pair, in the opposite direction. He seemed to be copulating with her as he relentlessly bore her down. If he noticed I was abducting his home, or if his teeth severed the connecting rope, my demise was as assured as hers.

Fortunately, neither eventuality occurred. I broke the surface and managed to heave my inheritance onto the lowest step. Then I gripped the edge before I started to sink again. I climbed slowly onto the stone and lay gasping for breath. The waters bubbled and seethed in subterranean fury as the beast discovered his loss.

An object bobbed by my side and I scooped it up and pocketed it. I pulled the rope and studied the gnawed end. Discarding helmet and boots, I dragged my prize upwards to a safer position. My gamble had paid dividends.

I was interrupted by a sob. Mother was standing at the door, poking the void with a torch. The beam settled on the chest's mossy lid. "You really are leaving!" she wailed.

I inclined my head. "I am going to college, to study theology. With diligence, I will learn why I was given the wrong gender. I may discover a purpose for my homo-sapphism."

"God will not aid you. He has hated you ever since you eructated in chapel. He will send you to limbo."

I pushed past her. I had never seen her so concerned for my soul. I chose a rucksack from one of the stuffed hitch-hikers in the lounge and filled it with the fruits of my treasure. I left a few baubles—pearls and gold teeth. I also packed a spare silk shirt and two of our nameless cats. By the time I was prepared, the sun—which is really female—had menstruated over the abominable horizon.

Mother clung to me as I made for the door. "After all this time! I will be lonely without you." I lunged for her breast, the unmilked teat, and sucked savagely. One for the road.

"I will invite you to my graduation," I promised.

"But what shall I do until then?"

I shrugged. "Learn the piano. Order a large coffin from Horam and re-assemble the soundboard inside."

"There is no metronome. The foot has finally gone off."

"I do not care about material things. I intend to devote myself to the mysteries of ontology."

She kept hold of my arm as I unslid the bolts. The door swung open to reveal the startled face of a postman. I was equally stupefied. Since the founding of the house in 1717 only two people had sent letters to our family: Adam Weishaupt and Basil Zaharoff. And both these had been examples of business correspondence. My namesake, the original Bartleby Cadiz, had started a small business exporting evil ideas to corrupt but unimaginative regimes—Syria, Haiti, Essex.

The postman handed me the epistle. It was addressed to mother. She opened it quickly, despite her anxiety, with an uncut thumbnail. It was from the occult savant in London, a reply to the request she had posted more than a decade previously. It claimed he was too busy with his own work to offer help. However, he enclosed a signed photograph for her to frame on her wall. She did not reveal his identity—a pathetic attempt to make me linger in her presence—but showed me the picture: a young man with oval glasses and a tweed suit.

It meant little, after all. I tipped the postman with a small ruby. He fled into the gnarled trees, his empty sack rippling on his back like a drained hunch. I made to follow him, into the real world, into mundane anguish and ridiculous absolutism.

Mother strummed at my limbs, her well-meaning malice as weighty as unplayable gongs. "After all I've done for you! What will you give me in return? Where is my recompense?"

I paused and stared up at her. It was as if I was seeing her black hair, her full lips and haughty brow, for the first time.

Wrecked on the coast of Hampshire during the Spanish Armada, moving inland and evading capture, our ancestors had chosen not to breed with the local denizens. They preferred to keep their genes private, mating with foxes and crows and moles rather than the English. It had kept our complexions sly and sultry, our motives hounded and earthy.

Without a word, reaching into my pocket, I offered her a symbol of my newfound independence. It told her everything I could not articulate verbally: that I no longer needed to suckle her shadows and substance, that I was capable of finding alternative nourishment, both mental and physical, in other corners of existence. She received it with a frown, recognising its obvious quality as a replacement metronome.

She nodded and rolled it in her mouth. It was the object which had surfaced in the cellar, the last item of the prostitute to survive. Stiffer than when attached to her breast, beautiful as a boil without a leper, pyramidal as an Ægyptiac riddle, tart as a bell dipped in vinegar, studded with nodules: a housewife's finest nipple.

I caught the first train from Horam's desultory station down to the soiled coast. Brighton, with its pavilions and strained bonhomie, was as welcoming as a milliner's run by a poisoner. It took to me instantly and in return I ensured I was not an ungracious guest.

My first act was the securing of false teeth, to replace those I had ground. The locals found my accent incomprehensible; nor could I make any sense of their dialect. Asking for directions to the nearest dentist, I was led by the hand to a hardware store.

Not suspecting a mistake, I strolled inside and pointed at my gums. The owner was bewildered by my request but proved himself an entrepreneurial fellow. He fitted me with a miniature gin-trap designed to snap the ribcages of pet mice, fully-sprung iron blades sharp enough to cope with the regional cuisine.

To be honest, the food did not trouble me: I was used to underdone morsels. Nor was the difference in latitude from my home injurious to my health. In all, I cut an intrepid dash, sauntering along the promenade, enjoying the sights and sounds of an alien culture.

Brighton was crowded with all manner of exiles: artists, writers and editors from the chilly Midlands. Physicists, philosophers and mathematicians from the wry towns of Kent and Surrey. Some of these could never return: their councils had passed the death sentence on them in absentia. But Brighton was generous to asylum seekers and only occasionally was I treated to the sight of a screaming bohemian being forcibly deported by customs officials. It was a frenetic place, healthy as a tumour.

With funds, life was easy. But my inner turmoil poured from my ears and nostrils. Even in the liberal clubs of this unabashed resort, among revellers and celebrants, my misplaced lesbianism found no valid outlet.

What use in slipping male fingers into a young girl's vagina? What point in kissing away her aureoles with manly lips? In supping her hair, toes or tongue? Only when she could reciprocate, matching caress for caress in exactly the same way, would I know true consummation.

Thus I held on to my virginity, relieving myself under the struts of the rotting pier, where the overpowering stink of dead fish served to delude me for brief moments as to the status of my own genitalia.

Following my original agenda, I enrolled in the renowned university as a theology student. Classes were held in the seminary wing, where the desks and chairs were stained with choirboy semen.

Even the books I was given bore the marks of onanism: pages were stuck together, covers crisp with innumerable layers of issue. The brow of our lecturer was varnished with two patches of ivory that rippled sickeningly when he frowned. I imagined the tiny sperm-corpses rolling over the waves, knocking against each other in the storm of his disapproval.

One afternoon, for a prank, some of the freshers dragged him to the Astronomy department and applied a spectroscope to his head. The blotches were revealed as emanating from different singers, soprano and contralto. The myth of his monogamy thus castrated, the lecturer became our slave.

The desk at which I sat was one of those outmoded affairs which can be swung open to reveal storage space. It was exceedingly voluminous and swallowed my bibles without chewing. Even a century of leaking choirboys had been insufficient to enamel all the wood.

Cryptic messages crawled along the bottom and sides, obscure insults from the past, splinters of gossip about long-decayed catamites. Not one of these runic confessions was pertinent to my plight. A normal appreciation of the opposite sex, let alone a perverse one, was totally lacking. The regime's flavour was Spartan in both senses of the word.

I applied to live at the Halls of Residence, but they were already crowded three to a cell. During my first term, I passed through a large number of bedsits, each as dismal as a cow's womb.

Finally I managed to obtain a place in a maisonette, sharing with one other. My flatmate was a medical student, impeccable in his manners, though with an irritating laugh which filled his mouth with mucus. Our first meeting was a mutual appreciation of outstanding defects.

I bowed deeply. "Bartleby Cadiz."

He mimicked the gesture, though with a rococo flourish, and took my hand. "Porlock Sniggervalue," he said.

Introductions over, we exchanged views on trivial topics. I stored my belongings and allowed him to conduct me on a tour of the dwelling.

All the time, his fingers were jerking nervously, as if they longed to hold a scalpel. He took his studies seriously: his own room was full of cages in which various animals shuddered. He had a genuine respect for life, shedding tears whenever a project demanded he dissect the beasts without the aid of anaesthetic. He was greatly enamoured of my nameless cats, baring his leg for them to sharpen their claws. We shared food, domestic chores and facile charisma.

He eschewed the local method of cooking, grilling everything until it confessed. Though he never went shopping, the larder was always full of victuals. My room was adjacent to the kitchen. In the early hours of one morning, through a hole in my door, I saw him replenishing the high shelves with fresh livers, his hands dripping with rabbit blood.

When I confronted him over breakfast, he merely shrugged. Wastefulness was the cardinal sin of his ethical system. I countered by pointing out that a diet of pure protein was unhealthy.

"But I'm a vegetarian," he protested.

I choked on my giblets and asked him to repeat his statement. He did so, without a flicker of hypocrisy.

"Refuse to touch meat. Horrible stuff, all stringy and obscene. My bowels won't tolerate it."

He was serious. I threw down my fork and spent the next hour using complicated syllogisms to convince him of his error. He was horrified, spearing a weasel heart with his knife and gazing at it intently. "You mean to say this isn't a vegetable?"

I nodded my head and picked my metallic teeth.

Still in a daze, he allowed me to lead him to the local market. The Brighton casbah was awash with picturesque characters, merchants selling candy floss and cheap shoes. In the greengrocer's quarter, I showed him the mounds of carrots and tomatoes.

Behind one stall, a portly man with a liar's beard sundered spinach with a cleaver. Green ichor splashed our clothes. Porlock paled and held a hand to his mouth. I could see that he was about to faint, and helped him to a nearby crate, where he sat with his head between his knees and retched alarmingly into the sawdust.

The stout grocer was amused. "Squeamish eh? Doesn't like to see the origins of roughage!" I took an instant dislike to him. His wares had an odd sheen, as if they had been grown in distant climes. Porlock was too ill to attend his classes, so I took him back to the flat and stayed by his side for the remainder of the day.

His soul was in a state of crisis. All his cherished notions about biology had been upset. His moral values had been torn to ragged strips by a metaphysical blade no less brutal than the one that had assassinated the spinach. He had considered himself a gentle pacifist living in harmony with nature. Now he knew himself to be a ruthless exploiter of fellow mammals.

I saw that he might injure himself in his anguish and I sought to console him. I remembered one of my lessons from the previous week and I recited its compelling arguments for his benefit. Slowly, he absorbed the wisdom of my speech.

"God wants us to harm animals. In his autobiography, he lists sixty different ways to torment a donkey."

Porlock looked up. "Will you show me?"

"The volume no longer exists. It was carried off millennia ago. But Hermes Trollope saw it and copied selected passages. In the Middle Ages, Fryer Bacon added an extensive commentary claiming that the torturing of beasts improves their flavour. Even Papus Levi concurs with this, citing coriander as an alternative. Abuse is holy."

The medical student was so cheered by my oratory that we continued into more profound theological depths. He wanted to know who had stolen God's autobiography. This was a Gnostic question, one still argued over by the most erudite scholars. I informed him that an evil spirit by the name of Gallico had taken it, in the form of a goose.

To be frank, this was the sum of my knowledge on the matter. Like a fever, his enthusiasm raised my temperature, muffled my head, turned my urine orange. He even toyed with the notion of changing courses. But I convinced him that God needed surgeons as much as bishops.

From that moment, whenever I returned from the seminary, I imparted the day's lesson to him, while he made notes. In tandem, his own studies reached a level where the college authorities permitted him to vivisect humans. We visited madhouses together to select victims. We had to order bigger cages, moving the rabbits into the bathroom. He always allowed me first incision, giving the leftovers to my nameless cats.

In return, on a rare occasion when he took a day off, I sneaked him into the seminary and concealed him in my desk. As he giggled with delight throughout the lesson, the lecturer may well have suspected his presence, but was too cowed to protest. When I opened the lid to retrieve him, his mirth had filled the whole space with swirling phlegm.

Undergraduate divinity rapidly solved most of his problems. I was less lucky. Not until the end of the second term did we begin to review aspects of love. Even then, I was left with a negative appreciation of my purpose in the grand sexual scheme. It seemed that God had scant use for women-lovers. I felt doubly cursed, like a crocodile trapped in the hide of an alligator.

I devoured the appropriate texts, reading banned manuals on procreation. Also, I sought solace in my favourite bible, a superb copy provided by the college. Bound in martyr skin, its flyleaf carried the names of all its previous owners—the first was Pope Joan. But even here the answers remained vague. I was unnerved by a notion that Porlock was attempting to outdo me in my own subject. The drains kept blocking and when I called in a plumber, he discovered volumes of Kierkegaard in the toilet cistern.

One evening, I returned home to find the rooms lit by candles. The atmosphere was one of heightened sensuality.

I moved into the lounge and greeted Porlock, who was dressed in a black kimono. He followed me into the kitchen: the table was laid and adorned with orchids. There was an amphora of clear liquid and two glasses. Before I could say anything, he touched my arm and whispered: "What did you learn today, dear?" This was so unexpected that the buttons on my shirt popped.

I stuttered through a synopsis of the lecture while he licked his lips. There were exactly two forms of love: carnal and spiritual. God valued both, though in the case of the first, his favourite position was unknown. It was essential that these desire-types were kept antipathetical.

Porlock chuckled softly. "What about Platonic love?" I could sense his mounting excitement. I pulled away and circled the table, placing it between us. I mumbled in confusion.

"I do not know what you mean."

"It is very elusive. Some say it cannot exist, that God has banned it from Heaven. Plato himself had doubts."

"I have never heard of this personage."

"A philosopher who lived in a cave illumined by sparks struck from the chains of slaves. Also, he invented crockery."

I sighed. "You have outstripped me in knowledge. Tell me about this third category of love and the mechanics of its operation. Why do others doubt its impingement on reality?" I feigned a purely cerebral concern, eager to maintain our customary abstract airs.

He leaned over the table and stroked the stem of the amphora.

"It lies midway between material and ghostly love. As such, it is euphoric but not excessive. It is the passion of twins who share a single set of clothes, the narcissism of a self-abuser without hands. It is the glory of mediocrity—chaste but not ascetic."

"This sounds an intriguing variant," I confessed uneasily. "Yet I have never witnessed an exemplar."

"It has an extremely short half-life. Within seconds it decays into eroticism or revelation. Plato judged it too unstable for this universe. In other dimensions, perhaps, it enjoys a vogue. The genius who is able to synthesise it here will be lauded for aeons. New industries will rise in the wake of his melding of base and holy."

I made a sudden decision. "I will be the one!"

His eyes glinted. "I think not. The task is beyond a mere student. Our emotions do not blend neatly, but swirl in paisley patterns, Allow me to demonstrate. At this instant, I am full of Platonic love. I feel for you what a mouth feels for its bite. But the emotion is fracturing even as I speak, reconstituting itself into its disparate parts. Carnal and spiritual elements are seceding."

With a lunge, he scuttled over the table like a scorpion and fixed my lips with a malignant kiss. Simultaneously, he rolled his eyes toward Heaven in a gesture of contrition. I could not see how these aspects had managed to congeal into one substance. But I did not doubt the sincerity of his speech.

I sought to wriggle free; he recalled his breath, holding me in the diplomacy of a vacuum. His tongue was sharper than a swallowed toad. His hands ranged as far as cellos. Had Homer embarked from his own isle to cross a wine-dark tablecloth and grope Sappho, inappropriateness would not have a better symbol.

My lame struggles were so foolish that he began laughing and broke the hermetic seal. His mucus crunched in my mouth. I spat and gaped at the multi-faceted phlegm. "Emeralds! You have been pilfering my store!" I was aghast at this treachery.

He coughed and spat more gems. "Did you expect me to rape you for nothing? Besides, hiding them inside your cats was too obvious. I gave the animals an emetic prepared from banjos."

I rushed into my room and discovered that my pets were completely empty. They caterwauled in precious hunger. Porlock was standing behind me. He stroked the nape of my neck: "Don't you want relief?" I rounded on him with my inbred fists.

Elusive Plato

After a prime number of ineffectual blows, he finally accepted that my reluctance to offer him my lower intestine was not merely the coyness of foreplay. I informed him that I preferred women, that I did not find him attractive. His face twisted in horror.

"You're a theology student! How can you be normal?"

"Do not mistake me. I am not heterosexual. I have perversions of my own, but I wish to keep them secret."

This admission satisfied him. He became more amenable. "I've spent most of the day preparing a romantic meal. No sense in letting it go to waste. We can still enjoy each other's company, without the involvement of semen or grace." I acceded and he added bitterly: "If only Platonic love wasn't so damned elusive!"

I took my place at the table while he manipulated a tin opener. It seemed a breach of etiquette to observe him; I turned from the theatre of operations. I heard the slither of vitamins and fibre, the friction of calcium. I wondered aloud what delicacies, what vital organs, he had torn from his thrashing charges in the doomed attempt to seduce me. The green of his laugh was tinged with blue.

"No viscera," he maintained. "The pain had to be mine. I wanted to prove the fanaticism of my lust."

"Vegetables?" I whispered in disbelief.

He grunted in the negative but my relief turned to terror when he added: "Even more wholesome."

Against my better judgment, I pressed the point. His forced gaiety shredded into existential dejection, like a defrosted nun pushed through a confessional grille. He spoke with considerable difficulty. Yet I did not look up even when he bore the dishes to the table. My nose informed my superego of the truth before my eyes had a chance to catch a single photon of the horror. Tinned peaches!

With grisly understatement, he said: "Fruit."

Before me, knocking against each other like drowned choirboys, like magnified amoebae, like flooded basilicas, like the guillotined heads of aristocratic sperm, the amber monstrosities gurgled under their bridal veils. The thin cream crashed on the bowl's chipped sides in wavelets surfed by my misery. The mock-purity of this desecration rushed into the deepest recesses of my unfurled cerebellum. I jumped up and heaved over the table, spilling skinned memories. Porlock regarded me with heretical fatalism—he already partly understood.

My will broke down and I clutched him for comfort.

"What's wrong?" he demanded.

As if a barrel of sour wine had been breached to baptise my unborn descendants, I felt awash with vintage and corrosive motives. I resorted to the desperate expedient of the truth.

"I am a lesbian," I replied.

At once, the blood shot to his face. Turning the colour of a boiled pornographer, he loosed a veritable torrent of phlegm and jewels. There was a rare light in his eyes. His fingers jerked and twisted. "Can it be a valid diagnosis? Why not! A lesbian trapped inside a man's body! What a moral dilemma! What a medical challenge!"

I had never seen him so reconciled to the disappointing cosmos. His expression reminded me of my sister, when we released her from her attic confinement. I relaxed in his arms, like a prisoner whose father is the hangman. Already, his shaking hands were exploring my form in a detached way totally at odds with his former passion. In response to my gasps of surprise, the nameless cats arched their backs.

"How do you feel?" As he roved my various corners, he followed each grope with a comment. Pinching the skin on my chest, he cried: "You need much more here." Then he was between my legs. "This must come off right away." For my own hands, his observations were highly reactionary. "And these must learn to clean and cook."

He picked up the amphora, which had retained most of its contents, and collected most of the peaches from the carpet. He filled a glass and bade me drink. I did so and gasped; the stuff was ethyl alcohol. He had obviously pilfered it from college. He poured me a refill and downed one himself. "To celebrate," he proclaimed.

Remarkable as it may seem, I had no inkling of his plans. I righted the table and we sat and imbibed, toasting each other with a sequence of impossible similes which lost sight of their original meanings and often stumbled into new ones. Soon I was half-blind and raving.

Porlock, whose colour had faded to that of a flayed newsagent, vanished and returned a minute later with a selection of glinting objects. I drained the amphora and hurled it against the fireplace.

The next twelve hours are a jumble of confused images. I recall, as wretchedly as if viewed from the end of an alimentary canal, the medical student lifting me onto the table and taking off my clothes.

His fingers tickled like fleas. Then he was lifting a tiny blade and lowering it and I felt I was being fellated by a mouse. The liquor had also impaired his sight and he held a magnifying glass over my besieged member. Was this a deliberate insult? I wondered.

The nameless cats were leaping all over my body. Porlock held a saw similar to the one mother had used to disembowel father's piano. Slivers of bone and fatty marrow sprayed over the wall. The candles hissed as my blood, rich as iron filings, showered the quivering flames.

I thought he was sawing off the table legs and chuckled; even when he held my marbled testes up to my face and cast them like dice before me, I sought merely to determine their value. Trouser snake eyes!

In frequent pauses between the stages of the butchery, he turned to the recovered peaches for refreshment. His determination to swallow them whole was admirable. I ranted my desire to join his unholy repast. There was something wrong with my mouth; I was unable to chew.

With a leer, he selected a bruised fruit, slid it between his molars and worked it to a mush. Then he fixed my lips in another unspeakable kiss and fed me like a deranged wet nurse, filling my throat with the mephitic slurry. I knew then that my false teeth had been removed.

My final coherent memory that night was of Porlock busy with needle and thread, nodding to himself. The world revolved around me as if I was the hub of the universe; I felt the room, the house, the town lurch over and under a fulcrum located between my eyes.

And beyond Brighton, oceans and mountains and other cities duplicated the gesture, more distant and thus spinning faster. And outside the world, the sun and planets, stars and numberless galaxies rose and fell in an unimaginable whirl. On and on, faster and faster, until God in Heaven, squatting on a throne baked from excrement and gold, was pulped to butter and—losing his seat in a mellow smear—thrown out beyond the limits of reality. Now the cosmos had to fend for itself. Olé!

I awoke from muddled dreams, still prone on the table. The nameless cats were beside me. They were reluctant to stir: they lacked heads. Who had decapitated them? I called for Porlock; he did not answer.

I climbed to the floor and staggered through the flat. My entire gait had changed, my hips rolling, my feet taking demure steps. I attributed this to the previous night's Bacchanal. I opened the door of Porlock's room, but he was not in bed. Catching sight of the carriage clock on his dresser, I wailed in horror. It was nearly noon; I had missed the morning lecture. I returned to my own room and started rummaging through my linen basket for the least odious of my silk shirts.

When I recovered it and tried it on, I was further confused by its poor fit. Usually my clothes billow like reluctant charity, clinging no tighter than a discouraged orphan. I maintain that sartorial space is an indication of probity and conscience. But this garment barely stretched across my chest.

My first thought was that Porlock had shrunk it in the wash of some practical joke; then I began to understand that my body had altered. I gingerly felt the ominous curves and angles of my anatomy. I was Bartleby Cadiz no longer! In a trauma of loathing and wonder, I fell toward the mirror on my wardrobe.

It confirmed my suspicions. My maleness had been stripped like the medals of a cowardly park keeper. What I had wanted in a spiritual sense had been granted to me on a lower level. There was a dark joy, a rush of ecstasy, but it was tempered with aesthetic objections.

Porlock had made a surprisingly messy job. The stitches warbled over my torso and thighs like strangled sobs. My stuffed hips were lopsided; my artificial vagina formed a sinuous curve; my breasts were lumpy and mismanaged. Even odder was the fact that whiskers radiated from my aureoles. I rubbed my vision into focus and approached my reflection.

My nipples were black noses. Porlock had ventured further than the changing of my gender. He had tried to convert me into not just a woman, but a housewife. This ambition had ruined the operation, leaving me with the appearance of a divorcee. I guessed he would want to exhibit me as a project and that his tutors would give him high marks for initiative but low ones for implementation. I wept for my nameless cats: overlooking no detail, Porlock had also widened my tear ducts.

Raising a leg, I treated myself to a closer inspection of my new sex. Parting the labia with some trepidation, I was greeted by an ecumenical hymen. The medical student had torn the flyleaf from my best bible and stitched it into the wound. Behind the translucent vellum, the shadow of my false teeth yawned. Had they been implanted as an example of Porlock's incisive wit? When I felt my throat, I traced the outline of a magnifying glass; the Adam's apple, citrus of Eden, had been removed.

I found it in the fruit bowl, an ornament always kept empty for the sake of Porlock's mental balance. In the larder, I chanced on my lingam, hanging on a hook with brother sausages. It was stuffed with masticated peaches and completely useless to me.

I resumed the tailored struggle, pulling my shirt as far around me as it would reach, wiping my twitching nipples on a sleeve and pulling on my trousers. They felt uncomfortable, without a member to rub against the stiff material. I would not be able to confront Porlock until he returned from college; I might as well try to attend my own afternoon session.

Stepping out into Brighton's gratified streets, I became extremely self-conscious. My world-view was in need of a radical overhaul. Rarely had I felt so threatened: tattooed men whistled at me from varied levels of scaffolding. Fingers pinched my behind. And women no longer regarded me with passionate abhorrence. But at last I was attuned to their sexual auras. I wanted to touch these women, to scratch them with my nails, to share feminine caresses.

The supreme irony was that they smiled, offered empathetic comments, openly admired my cleavage, but did not water with lust. Most women are not instant sapphists. No matter: time to seek them out later, in the waterfront clubs.

I crossed Victoria Gardens and negotiated Circus Street toward the ebon seat of academe. From this vantage the building resembled a rotting foot and the students leaning out of the windows were pale maggots ready to splash on the pavement below. The total effect was that of a Satanic metronome, marking time for the single jarring chord of life.

I entered the gates and to my dismay found the male students no less insolent than their uneducated peers. I was showered with degrading comments, twisted flattery and oppressive grunts. Had I been wearing a skirt, doubtless I would have suffered even more. Ignoring the abuse as well as I might, I reached the seminary wing, opened the door of my class in the middle of a lecture and took my place as quietly as possible. Heads swivelled on aching necks to drool at my entrance.

I sat and crossed my legs in the way that now seemed most natural, a higher angle than my previous norm. I wiggled my buttocks on my perch. My shirt parted like curtains and my nipples sneezed; at once there was uproar from the undergraduates. Many collapsed to the floor, clutching their groins. Puddles of foaming white liquid trickled from the bottoms of their trousers, merging into a Mare Masturbari. I thought the entire class was in danger of being swept into the corridors.

The tutor climbed his lectern and brandished his concordance. A ravenless Noah, he hurled the dove-white tome towards the dry land of my skull. It connected and bounced, bearing a twig of my psyche. But allegory is one thing, reality quite another: he did not manage to catch it on the rebound—evidence of the imminent grounding of his worries—but let it slip through his fingers into the milky slobber.

His courage, which had been slight since the spectroscope incident, now rose to the surface like a gynaecological bathysphere. He stamped a foot and bellowed: "A woman in theology class?!!"

His fury made it seem that he repeated the phrase many times. In post-coital shame, the other students took up his chant. More calmly, he pointed a finger at my feral bosom and added: "God will be very annoyed. He specifically asked us not to let in females. The rules are simple—no semen, no admittance to a seminary." I opened my toothless mouth to protest, to assert my identity as a genuine knowledge seeker. He refused to recognise me as a former pupil: I was an inanimate object.

With an unanimous howl, the students seized me and bundled me into my desk. In the roomy interior, I was thrown from side to side. What was happening? I realised I was being carried out of the college and through the streets of the resort. I stood and pushed against the lid; it would not budge.

The voice of my tutor came from above; he was standing on the furniture while his temporary minions followed his directions. "Straight down the Grand Parade! Keep going at the Old Steine! Cross Madeira Drive onto the Esplanade!" I could tell he was determined to enjoy a fugacious lick of power before his status reverted to that of vassal. I called for mercy, but my words were now those of a woman and thus not heeded. Salty odours penetrated my eschatological confines.

There was a pause and a muttered exchange. My heart—which Porlock had enlarged—pumped girlish blood around my considerate veins. We were at the entrance to the Palace Pier. My assailants were trying to obtain student discounts for tickets. After a minute of haggling, I was moving again, faster than before, as the mob saw their final destination.

There was a sickening lurch and I was tumbling violently within the desk, like a logical idea in the mind of a schizophrenic. My plight was accompanied by diminishing laughter. They had cast me over the side! Like many other women before me, I was being ignominiously dumped into chaos. I swore at that moment to recover my stolen inheritance and set up a foundation for the further development of misandry.

The impact stunned me, but I did not lose consciousness. For almost an hour, I lay in a daze. When I recovered the use of my limbs, I pushed against the lid afresh. This time it swung open and waves broke over the rim, dousing me with icy spray: I was at sea.

The pier was no more than a mile distant. I was drifting away from Brighton slowly enough to judge the local currents as mild. This eased my mind—I thought I could reach the shore without much trouble. As a female, I would have to employ the breast stroke instead of my customary front crawl, but I anticipated few technical difficulties. I was about to dive out of my scholastic coracle when I recalled that I was rather more than a standard woman. I had been converted into a housewife: impossible to swim more than a single stroke before sinking like a rhyming mechanic!

With this realisation came an acute hydrophobia. I trembled at the bottom of my vessel. The stains on the hull began to peel off, revealing pale orange wood. Soon I was surrounded by a slick of antique semen.

The irony of being stranded on a peach-hued raft in the middle of pietistic cream was not lost on me: I had been subsumed into one of my adolescent suppers. Further satirical aspects—a housewife having a meal prepared for her, an inversion of the natural order—hardly registered at this point. I was overwhelmed by the direness of my position.

For one thing, my island had started to take in water. The semen had caulked the hull, sealing the joints and porous teak boards. Was this bureau an academic analogue to my sister's coffin? I knew that by closing the lid, I could trap enough air to slow down the rate of leakage. But squatting in the bilge proved unbearably claustrophobic.

I decided to die with stoic grace. I ran my hands over my body, to bid farewell to those annexed regions I had not yet colonised. The taut skin of my breasts, covering the furry mammary glands, responded to my touch, rumbling like submerged timpani. I saluted passing seagulls with a mocking poem. I was the Postmodern Mariner, stopping to harangue each bird in three, to crossly bow and fire quarrels at their beaks. Barbed bolts of rhetoric dislodged feathers in abundance, as if from violated pillows.

A sudden fog rolled in, obscuring my view of the coast. Hours condensed, the sun faded to a jaundiced disc of rancid sperm. Again I wept, less like a housewife than a secretary. Tainted globules held my regrets to ransom, manacled in sodium molecules. Down with my faithless desk I went, mumbling my own eulogy.

The tramp steamer loomed out of the mist like an interview. I waved my silk shirt and hopped on one leg. My coracle floundered in the surge of its professional engines. A bearded figure was leaning over the rail. His voice was soft, as if he had been garrotted with gut from a musical instrument. The ship, with its rusty decks and smudged portholes, the crab-haunted seaweed which strangled it, resembled an antediluvian growth that had refused to fossilise. When sparks spluttered from the funnel, the total effect was as sordid as the death agony of a hanged house.

My desk knocked against the bows and ruptured. Before I could drown, I was thrown a lifebuoy. I wrapped my limbs around it and was hauled over the side of the ship. The bearded figure panted.

"You're as heavy as an applied scientist who writes ballads in his spare time. Are you a graduate?"

I shook my head and shivered. He continued to make small talk and I was plagued with the feeling I had met him before. Then it dawned on me. The grocer from Brighton casbah! He betrayed no sign of recognition; the operation had moulded my cheekbones and lashes. He took me down into the depths of the ship and introduced himself.

"I'm Captain Nothing. Forgot my surname on a long voyage from

Elusive Plato

Hull to Liverpool. Never managed to remember it. But I'm still looking, been through all the archives in London. I'll get it back one day. Best call me Marlow until then. I've got a liver of darkness, you see. I'm headed for Margate. You can rest in the engine room until we dock. A bit noisy there but plenty of potato peelings to chew on. What appellation should I use when seeking your attention?"

I curtsied. "Bartleby Cadiz."

He frowned. "Odd name for a woman. Are you a divorcee?"

This was too much. "A housewife," I corrected. His eyes glinted at this news and he took a renewed interest in my nipples. An instant bulge in his trousers made me regret my pride. I covered myself with my shirt, but this only seemed to fuel his desire.

"In that case, madame, I must ask you to join me in the galley for a proper repast. You shall, of course, share my cabin. A housewife! Now I understand your high specific gravity."

He placed an arm around my waist and escorted me to a narrow room, lit by vases holding the headlamps of abyssal fish. He drew out a chair for my benefit and I sat primly at a low table. I avoided his gaze and studied his uncouth attire. Since my operation, I had become fascinated by clothes. He wore stormy slacks and a sweater adorned with bobbles of wool. It gave him the appearance of the Ephesian Artemis. He moved into an adjacent cell and returned with bowls of salad.

I stared at the green tangle before me and prodded it with my fork. Some of the salad's cogs were unfamiliar to me. I wondered where he had obtained such exotic and peculiar dainties.

Eager to impress, he leaned forward and whispered: "I'm a smuggler. I run vegetables between Brighton and Margate. I stock up on some of the rarer ones. The hold is full of cucumbers!"

I had read about these curved plants in Papus Levi. They were worth twice their weight in coal—no cleaner source of energy had been found. I was astounded by the Captain's claim.

While I attacked the more familiar olives and lettuce, he stretched under the table and placed a gnarled hand on my knee. I sighed and tried to brush him away. I was developing a massive hatred for romantic meals. Now I was a woman would I have to endure more of these abominations?

Not discouraged by my coyness, he rattled the vinegar bottle suggestively. I nervously awaited developments. He pursed his lips and whistled a sickly melody, his beard curling like a salted slug.

"Oh, Bartleby! How enticing your gums look in this light! How firm and alluring your pectorals! No need to cower behind blushes, my little sea urchin! Impale me on your naughty spines!"

"But what will your crew think?"

He smirked. "Don't worry, I run this ship myself. Come and see. Our antics won't be disturbed!" Without waiting for me to finish my avocado, he took my hand and led me through the stomach of the steamer. We raced up ladders and along warped tunnels. At the bridge, he showed me the wheel, unmanned and lashed with strings of beans.

"Is that not dangerous?" I asked. Positioned beneath the wheel, the mouthpiece of a speaking tube slurped my words and rumbled them to every malnourished corner of the ship.

The Captain ignored my concern and beckoned to a door. "This is my cabin. I want to share my erection with you. It's a flourishing example. Been storing it up for years."

"Thank you, but I feel I must decline your offer."

He roared and snatched me around the waist. Then he carried me over the threshold of his room like an aubergine.

I was helpless in his grip. He threw me onto his hammock and turned me onto my stomach. Then he divested himself of trousers and underwear, leaving his tubercular sweater in place.

"God despises this position!" I wailed. It cooled his ardour not a smidgen—he literally tore my velvet breeches from my bloated buttocks. Then, with the minimum of foreplay, he lunged at my virtue with a barnacle-encrusted member. My hymen would not split; he withdrew in dismay.

"You're unbroken! Are you sure you're a housewife?" Before I could save myself further indecencies by answering in the negative, he settled the matter himself: "Your husband is celibate? Is he an accountant?" He made another unsuccessful lunge. This time the violence of the rebound wounded him. He retreated in consternation.

"God wants to keep me pure," I fumed. I struggled to dismount from the hammock, but he held me down.

"No he doesn't. I spoke to him last night—sailors have a mutual understanding with the Divine. I prayed for an end to my loneliness and he promised to send me a woman. Here you are! So the toughness of your hymen is just a minor setback. I have the solution in the secret drawer of my cabinet. A box of Marital Aids!"

He dashed to a corner of his room and rummaged in the compartments of a facetious piece of furniture. I jumped off the hammock again; once more he threw me back, threading the whiskers of my nipples through the netting and tying them in maritime knots. He brought a box over and cast open the lid. It was full of unusual vegetables.

"Dildos of Carthage!" he exclaimed. He selected the most modest—a jalapeño chilli—and eased it between my ill-cut lips. It barely tickled the flyleaf. He tried with a courgette. The second attempt stretched the vellum no further than had his lingam. With navigational precision, he worked his way through his collection, each vegetable graded larger in girth and length. I experienced the concupiscence of parsnips, leeks and marrows. The hymen withstood them all.

Finally, after failing to woo with a pumpkin, he brooded and wiped his effluvium-soaked brow.

"I don't comprehend this. Best have a closer look. That's strange! There appears to be writing on your maidenhead." He reeled off a list of names: "Pope Joan, Thomas Aquinas, Count Stenbock, Virginia Woolf, D.F. Lewis. What's the meaning of this?"

"I collect autographs," I replied lamely.

"I've had enough of your coquettishness. My clipper won't be denied access through your straits! I'll broach the hymen with a paper knife." He fumbled through charts and sextants, scattering them over the floor. "Lord, where is that rusty blade?"

The item in question was acting the part of a bookmark in the large Ship's Log. Drawing it from its pedantic sheath, he crouched and curtly probed my vagina, opening the envelope of my virtue as if it contained a tax demand. I squealed at this defilement—the loss of ersatz innocence is a rare event. His knife struck sparks from my iron teeth and he leapt back with a superstitious cry. "Madame Elmo's fire!" He crossed himself before my yoni. "Is there a lodestone in there?"

"Reach in and pluck the answer," I suggested.

His inherent greed overcame his caution. Without a word, he rolled up his sleeve and plunged half an arm into the opening. I lost no time mulling the consequences; I contracted my muscles and snapped the trap on his wrist.

At first he thought I was demonstrating a sexual trick, an Æthiopiac manoeuvre; then as blood gushed like a menstrual audition, he tried to extract his limb. I twisted and jerked my abdomen, tearing his hand like a peasant savaging a baguette. The ripping sinews sounded two notes of my father's blasphemous chord. Pulling away, stump sealed with congealed slime, the Captain screamed the third.

He stumbled out of the cabin, delirious with rage. Still looped to the hammock by my whiskers, I could do nothing to effect an escape. So I waited in risible bondage, alternately gnashing my gums and baying.

The Captain returned some hours later, arm bandaged in spinach leaves. Eight barrels of hatred glimmered in his coral-reefed eyes. He had changed his courtesy from smuggler's to buccaneer's— the ironed cruelty was a tight fit on his bulky psyche. Yet he swaggered carefully before me, brushing the dandruff of compassion from the shoulders of sadism. I expected the same mercy a beekeeper grants a wasp.

"I am ready to suffer horrid tortures," I lied, "but I insist on a final request: do not smudge my cosmetics."

To my chary relief, he announced that he was unable to conceive of adequate torments. "I must dwell on this matter for a week. Until then, I'll lock you in the hold like a sister."

He jerked me from the hammock, pulling whiskers from nipples, and dragged me out of the room and back through the passages. Even with one arm, he was stronger than I. He stopped at a hatch, lifted it with the toe of his boot and hurled me into the void. The greeting odour made it seem I was falling into a garden party.

I landed on a soft mound of tusks. The hold was full of cucumbers, nestling like tongues. I thrashed among them, sucking at random to ease thirst and anguish. The hexagonal inmates had a delicate flavour at odds with the boorishness of their bootlegger. When I was satiated, I made a quilt of their skins and slept soundly. I woke to watery caresses; like compound sperm, the vegetables were seeking to conjoin with me, deeming the yolk of my ego suitable mating material.

How was I going to escape? I was unable to reach the hatch even by stacking the green spears. I stumbled through the gloom and touched the side of the hull. Tracing its perimeter, I chanced upon the earpiece of a speaking tube. The ship was threaded with brassy conduits, a sclerotic nervous system.

I laughed and tickled myself; my genius sprang to my aid like an acrobat on a trampoline woven from grasshoppers. I picked up one of the fruits, rattling the latent energy within. It is well-known that cucumbers are repositories of sunlight.

Since my operation, the growth of my fingernails had accelerated. I raised them to my throat. Long as thumbs, sharp as worms, they sliced my flesh with feminine propriety. Gritting my gums, I plunged the calcified assegais into my neck and parted the drapes of my wound. Stitches popped and the scar reopened; I reached inside and grasped Porlock's magnifying glass. It came loose with a flood of lodged curses.

Focusing the cucumber with the lens, I directed a spot of harnessed solar radiation onto the other vegetables. They ignited almost at once. I was surprised to note they burned with a purple light—Papus Levi had insisted the glow was blue. Having said this, it must be remembered that he coaxed his fire by rubbing two cucumbers together.

Before long, the hold was a mass of writhing flame and coiling smoke. I pressed back from the flaring fruit, covering my mouth and eyes.

As planned, the smoke was rapidly drawn up the speaking tube. There was nothing more I could do but wait. Would my scheme succeed before my body barbecued? The senile bulwarks grew hot, singing my derrière.

After an age of anxiety, I felt the vessel pitch. As if from the far side of a bible, the Captain's voice roared imprecations. The angle of roll forced the flames to lean in the opposite direction, to avoid falling over. The cucumbers screamed indignantly as they blazed.

With savagely tender finesse, the ship ground upon unseen rocks. I gaped at the gash which opened in its side. With a brief phallic salute to the Divinity, I plunged through the hole and out into the night. One slip at this point and my housewifery was over.

I hopped between points of jagged boulders, picking my way to terra firma. Behind me, the vessel bellowed in disgust. Flames darted in my wake and licked the outer hull. Steam and smoke joined tendrils and danced joyously. Limpets broiled in their own shells, like syphilitic knights.

High on deck, Captain Nothing rushed to the rails and glowered down at me. "What have you done?" he cried. Though still clad in his bobbled sweater, his head was squeezed by a nightcap. If he was truly Artemis, I was Herostratus, who burned the deity's best temple some three centuries before God's son found a job. Surveying the damage, the fool gnashed and swallowed his beard. "How did you manage this?"

"By directing acrid smoke through the speaking tubes," I answered. "It emerged in the bridge, withering the beans which lashed the wheel in place. With a loose rudder, we were at the mercy of God. I knew he would direct us to shore, because maroons make loyal adherents. Also, he is constantly lobbied by divers for more wrecks."

"A Captain must go down with his ship. I invest you with authority to demote me to a lesser rank. Please!"

"That would be unjust. You have worked hard to attain your present position. Polish your beard for death."

"I have no surname. How will my soul cross into Heaven? The border controls have recently been tightened."

Shaking my head, I pointed out the inconsequential nature of human nomenclature. God kept genetic records of individuals. "Besides, it is not your soul which ascends—that is a common misconception—but your wallet. What use has God for ghosts?"

"My wallet is also nameless!"

"Then you are condemned to a nullity of unfathomable dimensions." I did not enjoy uttering this pronouncement, but the smouldering rogue let loose a howl of elation. He clapped his hands and started dancing. I was impressed by his graceful pirouettes.

"That's it! That's my name! Marlow Nullity!"

I retched at his misplaced jubilation. My final glance showed that his arabesque was alight and the ship was breaking up. Then I hopped to the safety of a pebble-strewn beach. White cliffs towered above me, rags used to mop a behemoth's sperm. I clambered a steep path to a prodigious vantage and rested under the roof of a sheep.

Dawn peeped in due course, breakfasting on the fields. I flounced through jam-pink dew and crested a rise. Below, an espresso town percolated.

Elusive Plato

I was in Dover. My extensive reading had included atlases of modern cartography. The position of the massive castle and museum, the Old Gaol and Roman Painted House, left no doubt in my mind.

My considerable gusto was diluted by the realisation I should not enter. Semi-naked and wholly bedraggled, I was no sight for the inhabitants of a naval garrison. Men were to be avoided, especially flared ones. I suddenly decided to return to mother's limpid bosom—to achieve this aim intact meant skirting all major centres of human population.

While I brooded on the apex of the cliff, a curious apparition came across the meadow toward me. It was a masked midget trailing a string of visors. I was tempted to stand aside and watch him fall—he was plainly a suicide.

But perverse pity urged me to pluck his cable and stop him in his tracks. I questioned his gargoyle features on the subject of despair and his apparent surfeit of it. But I had made an error: he was appalled by my assumption of his motives.

"Kill myself? I'm a successful artisan!"

"You are heading toward the edge of the cliff," I pointed out. "One more step and your bones will be littering the beach. Have you ever seen a lobster hatch inside a skull?"

"I thought I was progressing in the direction of London. I plan to attend the brutal hunt—the *venatione*—in Highgate. Great opportunity for hawkers. I'll sell my masks at triple price."

I frowned. "Explain more fully."

"Are you a foreigner? The *venatione* is the epitome of the Capital's year. A menagerie of beasts are let loose through the streets—horses, boars and giraffes. Starved lions pursue them in relays. The Pope shoots the survivors with a musket."

"This sounds a most instructive spectacle."

He tapped his porcelain cheeks. "I'm wearing one of my products, to tempt potential buyers on the road. Unfortunately, I didn't have time to bore eye holes. Keep losing my sense of direction."

Impetuously, I cried: "Let me lead you! I am also travelling toward Highgate. I lost a large sum of money recently and wish to recoup funds. Are the prospects in the Capital good?"

"Depends on your métier. Housewives can earn plenty in the bagnios. Divorcees are less in demand. What are you?"

To preclude further harassment, I declared: "A virgin."

"In that case, I suggest you join the Guild of Ushers. Can you heft a halberd? The Guild are responsible for herding the beasts. They always need fresh blood. Virgins are becoming scarce."

"What are the wages like?"

"Nine amethysts an hour. The Guild used to provide accommodation as well—a tiered mansion lit by torches."

"The House of Ushers?"

He nodded. "That's the one. It fell down."

It seemed better to postpone my family reunion and return to mother only when I had rebuilt my fortune. Gainful employment was something new and fascinating. I would save my wages and invest them wisely. It would be a profitable experience in other ways: a chance to interact with the lower classes and observe their behaviour. Perhaps then I might re-enrol in college to study Anthropology or Ethnography.

There was one stain on my optimism—the possibility the Guild would reject my broken hymen and leave me penniless among strangers.

I confided my worry. "I am the victim of a shipwreck. The accident robbed me of my virtue and brassière."

"The loss of a hymen is no problem. Not all virgins have an intact seal; often they tear them on seesaws. The Guild knows this. But lack of a brassière is a serious disadvantage."

"Might I borrow two of your masks to cover my exposed breasts? This will serve as a novel support and will advertise your wares to a broader audience. My bosom is misshapen but pert."

He saw the sense of my suggestion and selected a pair of cat faces. They were a perfect fit. Tying the remnants of my tattered shirt around my waist, I contrived to make a respectable figure. In gratitude, I took the artisan by the elbow and steered him between ewes.

We tramped fields and drover's lanes until noon. Managing to sell a visor to an innkeeper, we secured two mugs of ale and a wedge of cheese. In my modest outfit, I was treated chivalrously by the other patrons—we traded two more masks and filled a hessian bag with provisions.

On the long journey, the midget, who gave his name as Cobalt Hugh, kept up a constant babble of anecdotes and tall stories. He was from the Continent—a tiny republic on the far side of Switzerland. A voluntary exile, he had worked as a popular composer; while thrumming a balalaika he chanced upon a chord so wretched it made a mockery of entertainment. Music was impossible after that; he fled across the English Channel, in the belief that chords cannot swim. Now he was a vendor of dominoes and pantomimic garb.

By the time we passed Canterbury, I had twice digested the entire story of his miniaturised life. His other tales were muddled folkish pieces. He recounted the drab adventures of an arrogant cockerel who broke a fox on a wheel and jabbed him with a heated poker.

While he sought to amuse me with this nonsense, real events of a remarkable nature were occurring around us. A genuine highwayman, echo of a smellier age, threatened me at a crossroads with a packet of ginger biscuits; a house shaped like a hat loomed to one side, brim occupied by a man playing a saxophone; a faded harlequin armed with an arquebus threaded through the trees. The artisan was oblivious to all this, continuing his rambling foolery.

I started muttering inaudible prayers. I asked God to rid me of the shrunken bore. For some reason, he would not oblige. Sleeping in a glade one night, I dreamed that Heaven was in mourning—I saw a procession of angels in top hats and dark suits. When I awoke, I collected belladonna leaves and brewed a poisonous tisane for my comrade.

In the morning, he drank it unquestioningly and licked his blue lips. The dosage was enough to induce a heart attack in a troll. It should have finished him within a minute. But his heart was too small for death to find. The marauding toxins galloped past it without a glance.

A fortnight later, after brief sojourns at Faversham and Rochester, we broached the outskirts of the Capital. The muddy alleyways and rotting bridges, the chaotic markets and riotous taverns belied everything I had heard. The streets were not paved with platinum. Chimneys protruded at toppling angles from decaying factory roofs like the ears of pernicious rabbits. The polluted Thames was awash with dead hogs and buskers.

Now I understood Papus Levi's buoyant housewife—without

God's permission, nothing could sink in that slurry. Reluctant to venture on the unstable bridges, we took a ferry from Greenwich to the Isle of Dogs, paying the bargee with a mask in the shape of a waiter.

The native women were loose but aloof. They favoured short skirts and stockings, but did not appreciate comments on hems and sheerness. I guessed my lesbianism would remain theoretical until my purse matched my breasts in radius. Seduction was expensive in the metropolis. Because of his size, the artisan preferred to flirt with rats and pigeons. All his efforts were unsuccessful—pressing his suits resulted in nothing more than creaseless frustration.

"Perhaps you should also join the Ushers?" I remarked.

He took this as a slur on his condensed masculinity, waving a fist and rigorously denying his virginity.

Entering Highgate in a state of mutual disenchantment, we formally bade each other farewell. He wanted me to return my masks. His pettiness threatened my future; uncovered breasts would not be granted an audience with the Guild. Stubborn as a phobia, he repeated his demand. He reached upward to snatch my mammary supports.

On a cruel impulse, I whistled a high note and struck my grimacing brassière. Each cat face sounded a different pitch. Together, the three tones constituted my father's elegy. "Was that your chord?" I asked. He shuddered and his porcelain visor burst into shards.

The visage beneath the covering was identical—pinched and improbable. Iced by gargantuan sorrow, he slumped in the gutter. I bowed sardonically and deserted him with feminine justification.

Making my way to the ruins of the House of Ushers, I clambered over debris and gained the Personnel Department: a solitary desk in the gutted shell of a hall.

The examination was conducted with brisk efficiency. There were no forms to fill out—virgins are poor spellers. A blonde girl considered my application. "Are you experienced?"

"Of course not! My hymen ruptured on a seesaw."

"Your brassière is very commendable. But do you know how to torture animals? Can you sharpen a pike?"

"I have read God's autobiography. I once made a noose out of an eel and hung an owl. I have Spanish blood."

Elusive Plato

As she measured my waist and inside leg, I studied her nose. It was a struggle to keep my nipples from hardening—the beauty of her profile was excessive. She had the bone structure of a niece but the brows of an aunt. Shortly, to my repressed relief, she shook my hand and welcomed me as a new member of the Guild. The *venatione* was due to take place in one week; I had to undergo an intensive period of training. The prospect of sharing bunks and showers with fellow virgins bathed me in a corybantic fulgor. My labia moistened in approval.

In the grandiose remains of the mansion, tents had been erected. I was taken by the blonde to meet my colleagues. The Ushers were gathered around a bubbling pot on an open fire. Lances and pole axes were stacked into ziggurats. Freckled redheads greased tridents while burly brunettes ironed uniforms. Lines of latent sexual energy radiated like scythes on a barbarian chariot.

So many virgins in one place was tearing the fabric of reality. The nuptial bedsheet of destiny was pining for a drenching. But the camp was run with such demure competence that God had obviously chosen to overlook its unnaturalness. Possibly my sapphic fingers could help to relieve the virtuous pressure.

I was handed a bowl of asparagus soup and a slice of prepubescent bread. I fitted into camp life like a spider into a glove—three of my desires had to be lopped. But the others were catered for with the cool efficiency of a military convent. My trainer, a strong-ankled girl who looked like a tennis player, handed me a javelin and ordered me to rush a stuffed fox hung on a hook from a lopsided wall. I complied with the skill of my youthful training, when I had impaled gnats in flight with thorns.

The recruits were unanimously impressed by my performance. The Cadiz family, I informed them, had learned all there was to know about thrusting weapons while fighting the Swiss in the battles of Cerignola and Marignano. They applauded my heritage.

At the end of the day, we were allowed to relax and braid our hair by moonlight. My comrades were earthy and callow at the same time. Talk was bawdy enough—bets were laid on whether the Pope's vestments would be spattered with brains or just blood. Many spoke fondly of home, shoes and henna. The virgins came from all counties save Essex, which suffers a maiden shortage.

During my brief stay with them, fighting with pillows in crowded tents, sharing biscuits and gossip, holding hands and sipping wine, I began to appreciate them as real people, who had almost as much right to exist on Earth as I did. I loved them all; I wanted to pleasure each and every one.

Because of this excess of choice, I dithered, making no seductive overtures. I licked not so much as a brunette's nipple, let alone played drums on a redhead's hymen.

Soon my chance had dissipated. The evening before the hunt—a last opportunity to touch knees or taste napes—the blonde Personnel Officer made a bombastic speech, praiseworthy but highly soporific. My potential lovers were bored frigid by the archaic flourishes. They would sleep now with dry thighs and inverted aureoles; I had lost them. My sighs fell in such knots that not even monkeys could have untied them.

The blonde kept her most coherent paragraph for the finale. I was aware that she studied my breasts intently as she delivered it.

"Remember to let nature direct your blows, my virgins! Why has God given animals markings? It's because he's a considerate deity! He wants the lance to strike true, the blood to spurt in charming rivulets. Like the torturers of old, who poked and prodded exactly where God told them to, we must not deviate from the ordained cruelty. Our Father knows the best way to prolong agony. Aim for the designated targets, the spots on the hide, and the day will suffer smoothly."

We had heard this before. My colleagues closed heavy lids over eyes in which dreams were already rehearsing. Even if I were to run my hands between legs and over breasts, I doubted there would be much moistening or hardening. Around me, vaginas were yawning. A single wakeful clitoris was not to be found in our ranks. After the speech, their owners limped back to their tents and chastely curled.

I was left alone with the blonde. Her vision was still attached to my bosom. I feared she wanted to share more truisms with me, unloading her basket of unused platitudes.

She smiled gently. "Bartleby, did your ancestors also fight against the Swiss at Bicocca in 1522?"

"No. By then we had switched sides. The Cadiz family always favours the underdog. Machiavelli noted this."

"I suspect you're looking forward to meeting the Pope? Only virgins can embrace him without haemorrhaging."

"My ardour for his holiness is tempered by the fact that he did not reply to any of my childhood letters."

"Your stubble looks very attractive under the stars. If you weren't Spanish, I might conclude you were a man in disguise. I venerate bearded females. Would you care for a drink?"

I declined her offer. I was so irritated by her interference in the seduction of my comrades that I did not perceive her words as an attempt to make advances toward me. This hideous irony only sounded the knell of my frustration long after she was abed. I crawled out of my tent, but it was too late. The horizon's own yoni was opening—the signal for mortal women to close theirs. A smutty sun leered.

It was the dawn of pain. Later, we marched down Hornsey Lane, the slap of our sandals on the cobbles providing the rhythm for our hideous Guild song. Crowds lined the pavement, strewing bunting and braying. At the end of the street, we entered Highgate Cemetery, the starting point of the hunt. Marquees and stalls had been set up around the beast cages.

I thought I glimpsed the midget, arguing with a customer over the price of a mask moulded like a harpy, but I was possibly mistaken. London was full of dwarves and stunted types—a product of malnutrition. Much of the populace existed solely on gin and tonic.

Standing on a portable dais, resplendent in his robes and rings, an antique blunderbuss crooked over one arm, the Pope issued blessings. His experience of such events was unequalled. Every day of the solar year, a different European city held a jubilee. Abandoning politics and charity, the Pope now devoted himself exclusively to attending these fairs. Some said he had killed half a million horses, filling the Vatican with their heads and boiling them to make glue. Sceptics questioned the need for so much adhesive. Yet it was true that the leaning tower of Pisa had ceased its relentless topple.

At any rate, he was a genial figure, full of love for his followers and a boon to taxidermists. It was difficult to resent him for the appalling decline in official bulls and excommunications. To each pontiff a new infallibility.

Starved for a month and beaten with poodles, the lions were in fine form. The lesson of the Florentines had been absorbed: the first revived *venatione*, in 1459, had failed miserably when the pampered cats lay down and fell asleep. For this reason, the Popes rarely said

Mass in Florence and had forbidden Brunelleschi's dome to be mentioned in guide books. At each brutal hunt, the city sent envoys begging the Vatican to repeal its grudge. The present Pope was considering absolution.

One by one, we were introduced to him. I was extremely nervous as I kissed his toes; looking up, I saw him rubbing at his member through his trousers. He had ordered the Turin Shroud to be made into Oxford bags; his bulge turned the image of God's eldest son into a monster, victim of an accelerated plague. The pontiff's drool washed my cleavage. I mewled.

After the Ushers were introduced, his holiness blessed the crowd in a variety of languages, including Welsh and Romansch, loaded his carbine with rosary beads and fired it into the air.

This was the signal for the release of the quarry. Horses, boars and giraffes bolted down the narrow cemetery paths, between the rows of bawling onlookers. It was considered sporting to give them a decent headstart. A string quartet rasped savage compositions and flicked its collective fringe.

The task of the Ushers was to pace the hunted and shepherd them down the appropriate byways of the course. Deviation from the route was deemed unlucky for the Guild. Pike levelled, I followed a knot of pigs and poked them about official bends and over anathematised graves. My fellow virgins chose their own beasts and demonstrated similar skills.

The *venatione* was run widdershins, against the sun's spiral, around the whole of Highgate. From the cemetery to Upper Holloway was the first stretch; then north-east to Crouch Hill; from here, a sweeping arc would take the hunt to Cranley Gardens, into Queens Wood and west to the limit of Hampstead Golf Course; then a broad rush down the notorious Heath and we would be back where we started. Any animals which had evaded the jaws of the lions— there were usually a dozen—would then be quelled by the Pope in an orgy of sparking flint and billowing gunpowder.

The difficult part of the route was the initial tangle of streets between Chester Road and Zoffany Street. If a quadruped was going to evade an Usher, this was where it was going to do it. Like a busker's song, blowing in the filthy wind, a terrified hog has little sense of direction.

A few of the animals had no idea what was happening.

Wandering in a daze, they nibbled grass on the verges of political tombs. An Usher must know how to cause pain without killing—some of my comrades let emotion compromise restraint.

A virgin I had spoken to on a number of occasions, a seemingly level-headed girl, was overcome by the texture of blood. The distinction between violence and lust had eroded in her geological mind. I saw her looming over a prone mare, inserting a phalanax-worth of pikes into its sweaty flank. Within a couple of minutes the unfortunate mount resembled a fakir betrayed by his bed. The virgin, whose glasses steamed with condensed ichor-vapour, loosed an orgasmic cry. A dark flood washed her thighs; her nipples pierced her toga.

This was a sacking offence. As she slumped in shameful contentment, the blonde Personnel Officer rushed forward with a suitable bag. Bundled inside, with a selection of worms, the offender would be slowly devoured by the invertebrates. It made sense to ingest quantities of vermifuge in the weeks preceding a *venatione*. I had been careful to take precautions, obtaining the worm-deterring drugs from an illicit pharmacist in Magdala Avenue. Not that I intended to break rules, but I knew the hunt's thumbs might unlace my inhibitions in like fashion.

The profane virgin begged for mercy as the Personnel Officer hauled her from the scene of her orgasm. She protested that the Guild's Code of Conduct was too harsh for a maiden who knew the names of so many shrubs. The blonde shook her sack. "Squirm but fair!"

As we trotted along, keeping the animals onto the designated track, the crowds started to thin out. They had been thickest at the holy axle of the Pope and among the melange of stalls. Here, spectators with less catholic tastes lingered, calling the odd word of encouragement.

When I was out of earshot of the fallen virgin's pleas, I relaxed somewhat and indulged the luxury of studying some of my observers. Families hampered in a double sense—with children and picnic baskets—sprawled on the grass like domesticated crop circles. In the hierograms of their lower class positions, I read a chronicle of quiet anguish and Sunday suppers every bit as horrid as my own. Tinned peaches seemed to hiss from tracts of sunburnt skin—amputated sopranos.

Near the gates of the cemetery, a group of Anglican vicars shouted iconoclastic insults. There are always a few extremists eager to spoil a Pope's fun. "Hunt children, not animals!" they cried. "Death to wafers! Death to waifs!" I tried to ignore them as I pursued a boar between the legs of a portly rector. He lunged at me with a revised edition of God's autobiography—the Sublime Vulgate. "This ritual is redundant. When are you going to start chasing orphans?"

I refrained from answering. A taller fellow, his dog collar stained with weird juices, snatched my brassière. "Fie! This is mortal heresy. I have never witnessed such a cataphysical undergarment. Remove it at once and prostrate your glands." He leered and spittle fled his sentences. My enlarged heart knocked on the door of my ribcage—I fell back and threw my hands over my seductively kohled eyes. I recognised my attacker as an archetypal enemy of the Cadiz dynasty.

I have already stated that my artisan companion, the midget, was an exile from a mountainous republic in the Alps. Before meeting him, I was aware of only one other exile from that place. In Horam, on the far side of town, a vicarage squatted amid the famed cider breweries like an incontinent gardener. Marigolds and petunias and amnesiac flowers lurked in the fibres of trellises—they warted the walls. The entire religious complex, with the little attached chapel, exuded such an air of starched oppression that our family rarely ventured into its environs. Thus cider was an unknown taste to our toad's tongues.

The occupant of this tyrannical building was a fanatical parson who licked pennies from his collection dish and dried linen on his lightning rod. Despite being a newcomer to the village, he denounced our adherence to the True Faith as if he was fighting the original Armada. Fiery as a burning fairy, he preached against my father's Bösendorfer, urging the Council to confiscate our sacred relics—including the stuffed labia of Jeanne d'Arc, a gift from Napoleon.

There was something fascinating in his monumental fringe— mother once invited him for supper. Refusing to attend, he hammered a document to our door which outlined ninety seven reasons why we should pack our gilded chests and return to Spain. His pulpit was a flaccid phallus carved from yew and varnished in Earl Grey. He took two sugars with his halitosis.

His name was Douglas Delves and he was almost never seen

without a pickling jar the size of a pig. This jar was kept always covered and it was a mystery as to what it held. Some said his wife; others claimed it was the repository of his belief and that if it shattered he would turn agnostic. At any rate, this was the first time I had witnessed his back unburdened by the glassy container.

He did not associate the fair maiden before him with the youth who trained vipers to copulate with his garden gnomes. As I wrestled to free my brassière from his clutches, the hog I was pursuing ran off the route at a snorting tangent and into the midst of some peripheral picnickers. As large as a pickling jar, it caused great havoc amongst the sandwiches and sausage rolls.

I groaned and smote my forehead. If these spectators lodged a formal complaint, it might endanger my status in the Guild. Our motto—*Video Meliora Proboque, Deteriora Sequor*—was an ironic comment on Ushers who had been defrocked for just such an offence. The Personnel Officer, now I had shunned her amorous approaches, would care little for my excuses. The hog was my responsibility.

Lifting a teabag out of his pocket, the Reverend Delves swung it on its string and popped it into his mouth. Addicted to caffeine, he sucked the juice out of the leaves and spat the dehydrated bag onto the ground. Then he renewed his assault on my breasts.

I saw he was close to peeling off my mammary supports and raised my pike to defend myself. But these weapons are unwieldy at close quarters. The other Anglicans roared with merriment at my ineffectual attempts to plunge the point into the Reverend's neck. At last, I resorted to words. Glaring into his simian eyes, I said calmly, "Sir, your pickling jar is having an affair. You are a cuckold."

My desperate stratagem worked; he opened his mouth, dribbling cold tea, and relaxed his grip. "Do you know me? Who are you?" He studied me more carefully, but Porlock had been thorough. To all appearances I was an authentic Usher, a real virgin—there was more of the Seville about me than the Cadiz. Tears crowding under his lids, he added: "My jar is unwell. That's why she's absent!"

I sighed. "Always the owner is last to know. Even now, now, very now, an old black carafe is topping up your white jar. I am one, sir, that comes to tell you. Your receptacle and the flagon are now making the beast with two bungs."

He howled and nibbled his fingers. "This accident is not unlike my dream. Belief of it oppresses me already." He tugged at his dog collar, gasping for breath. "When I find them, I'll reconcile her to Heaven and stopper her neck with a cushion. My parishioners will speak of one that pickled not wisely but too well."

With this archaic vow, the Reverend Delves fled through the gates and was soon lost in the general traffic.

The portly rector who first harangued me jabbed a puffy thumb. "You vestal Jezebel! He travelled from Sussex to attend this demonstration. I doubt he'll ever leave his vicarage again!"

My inconsequential reply was drowned by another carbine blast. This was the signal for the releasing of the lions. I brushed past the rector and retrieved the hog, urging it out of the cemetery with hasty thrusts. The starved cats would catch up with the stragglers very quickly indeed. They might be distracted briefly by the picnic baskets or the picnickers themselves, but generally they would follow the trail of blood spilt by the Ushered prey. Growls tore the air.

Already in the distance I could discern a frenzied lion running up a path, tongue dragging in the dust, lapping the dripped gore. There was a bonus for the Usher who managed to herd the greatest number of hunted beasts back to the starting point.

Panting down Sandstone Place, I drove my charges around the first tight bend and into the sentient litter of Bredgar Road. There were very few onlookers here; people leaned out of windows like beflunked students. The scattered newspapers and remains of greasy food undulated as the pigs burrowed beneath sheets of filth. This avenue of diabolical ordure might confuse the lions for a moment. Noses weep and eyes sneeze in this part of London.

Turning left at the sewer's end and proceeding toward Archway Mall, we greeted the confusing tangle of small streets where many Ushers come to grief. I dipped into Giesbach Road and wheeled into short Boothby, a thoroughfare with the same temper. Were they brothers? I lost a pig at this juncture—it snorted off in the opposite direction. Impossible to retrieve it without sacrificing the others. Lions seemed to be roaring ahead of us; doubtless a trick of the thin streets, warping acoustics. My nerves tightened an octave and the pike shook in my hand. My terror smelled of truffles, calming the hogs.

Passing a row of abandoned buildings, I considered the

feasibility of cheating. If I concealed my hogs in a deserted office until the lions passed, I could wait until the final stages of the event and then slip back into the cemetery to claim the bonus.

It was not beyond my cunning. It would mean disguising the largest pig as my husband and the others as our children. Who would suspect a typical lower class family arriving at the end to catch the Pope's contribution? Once inside the gates, hidden behind a pompous tomb, I could remove the disguises and reveal myself as the winner. A suitable daubing of sweat, a couple of apt comments about the extreme length of the course and the prize would be mine. Who would deny such an obviously dedicated damsel?

This seemed the undertaking most in keeping with the Cadiz name. In Grovedale Road, I chose a tenement leased to solicitors and actuaries. I pushed at the front door—not gingerly, which is a fool's way, but with fingers like chillies. The edifice was a baroque semi-ruin, the interior walls smothered in calendars depicting ridiculous nudes.

Ceilings sagged in a fashion that made me mourn my bosom's future—my breasts would not always be so sprightly. It was difficult to imagine workers keeping hold of their sanity in these conditions.

Strange machines lurked in every corner of the room. These included water dispensers and portable fans. Other devices were of a more dubious character: appliances for driving staples through fingers or for forging multiple copies of incriminating genitalia.

All this memorable equipment was powered by clockwork—I wound the mighty springs for amusement. Not every machine jumped into action; a few had hidden triggers I was unable to locate. When I had satisfied my curiosity, I turned my attention to a more urgent duty—praying that the lions would not trace our scent into the building. I had little desire to mop blood with insurance claims. To die in an office is to rubber stamp your soul.

The hogs were lively and refused to hide in wastepaper baskets. The unwounded ones climbed over the whirring contraptions. It was impossible to calm them. Nervously, I barred the entrance with a filing cabinet and peeped through the venetian blinds.

A grovel of lions—too matted to be a pride—loped past, nostrils streaming. They did not look up or sniff at the tenement. I relaxed in a swivel chair and rested my feet on a desk. I was pleased with myself and rubbed my palms with tender vigour.

"Oh, Bartleby! If you were not already me, I would propose wedlock! What better spouse could there be?"

My narcissism was interrupted by a loud squeal. The largest pig had fallen into the paper shredder. Another had managed to start the inhuman gadget. The unfortunate omnivore—a pork document vital to the workings of my scheme—was ripped to scratchings by the small blades. I had lost a potential husband! I was a single parent! I jumped up to offer comfort to the father-spattered children.

"Oh, pretty warty ones! Oh, my abusèd hogs!"

In swinish grief, they stamped around the workplace, knocking over lamps and potted plants. The vibrations of hooves on floorboards was too much for the senile office. With the gasp of a pounded receptionist, the ceiling gave way. Plaster and joists tumbled and crushed the mourners. I ducked under a desk and preserved my wonderful life. Dying pigs leaked a foul ichor: soon the room smelled like a functioning office. I vented my sorrow as a woman—shedding more water than I had ever imbibed. Without living beasts to usher, my prospects were dire.

By this time, my fellows would have gained a salient advantage. Not only had I lost the certainty of winning the bonus, but had jeopardised my chances of even finishing the course. My solitary hope was to return outside and pick up stragglers which the lions had missed—an unlikely prospect. Then I would have to sprint the entire loop. To come last is a dreadful humiliation for an Usher and whoever earns this distinction has to forego the Pope's ceremonial grope.

With a weighty spleen, I crawled over the rubble and staggered back into the open. Lions had left bloody footprints over the pavement; bones steamed in the gutter. Dragging my pike, I followed the spoor to the end of Ashbrook Road, my sandals slipping on the innards of chewed stallions and geldings. Trailing the hunters proved ghastlier than preceding them. The knowledge that my breasts were related to these killers, in the same way that axes are cousins to cleavers, filled me with nausea. I jumped a wide selection of equine viscera and manes.

While accelerating up Fairbridge Road, I was startled by a flash of ochre from a side-street. I stopped in my tracks and blinked— something was trotting casually toward me. To my utter amazement, it turned out to be a baby giraffe. This was a stroke of luck more welcome than that of a gambling masseuse. I crossed myself fervently.

The giraffe noticed me and returned my ravenous gaze with a spotted curiosity. I coiled my tendons to spring.

My desperate rush was poorly executed and gave the creature time to register the threat. Biting off its blue tongue in panic, it revolved on its own axis and bolted. Taking careful aim, I threw my pike with all my might—it was not a javelin and span ludicrously through the air, blunt end connecting with the giraffe's neck.

The camelopard wobbled but did not collapse; it gave a disturbingly human cry. This yell became an ambiguous sigh as I mimicked my weapon's trajectory, neglecting only to rotate. The silly mammal sought to evade my evil arms, retreating into the shadows of Courtauld Road. I retrieved my pike on the hoof and punted with it as far as Elthorne Park, a tangle of verdant drunkards where the giraffe sought sanctuary. I called to the creature with a sibilant tongue.

"Señor Giraffe, there is no escape. You must die today. Do one good service before losing your elongated life: help me to win first prize. I shall nibble a leaf in your memory."

This speech, made more for my benefit than my quarry's, was greeted by the giraffe with a sardonic bow, almost as if it understood my words. Then it was off again, weaving between the stunted trees and leaping the railings onto Beaumont Rise. I followed quickly but it took care to stay out of range of my best cast. Not so dumb a beast as my books had led me to believe! Giraffine stupidity was proverbial; now I was learning about the greater stupidity of proverb makers.

The tireless camelopard led me a gloomy dance up Cromartie Road and around Hornsey Rise Gardens. Then we were in the midst of some overgrown wasteland, a ribbon of nettles and wild parsley which tied Highgate like an unwanted parcel.

As I waded through the tall grasses, I was aware the giraffe was waiting for me. It actually wanted me to catch up! Surely it was not enjoying the hunt? Perhaps it deemed the *venatione* a furious but essentially harmless game? More likely the brute was a lunatic— indeed, it did seem to have mooning eyes. No matter: I would make craters of its spots and eclipse its selenodontic arrogance.

"Señor Giraffe, an awakening both rude and melodic is in store. Six punctures in your throat and with each breath you will play a flute back to my triumph. A Pied Piper leading himself!"

This pledge coupled with baser verbal abuse served to expel poisons from my lungs which were giving diplomatic immunity to the breath I was trying to catch. But while I oiled my viciousness, the baby giraffe gave a snort indistinguishable from a laugh.

At that instant, two anomalies in the situation finally assailed my brain. The first was that young animals are banned from such hunts—the sport is too easy. The second was that, according to my finest bestiary, the giraffe is the one totally silent mammal in God's repertoire.

It was possible to explain the latter by casting doubt on accepted learning—a camelopard might simply never have uttered a chuckle for the eardrums of an ancient natural philosopher. But the former discrepancy was a lankier issue; before me, unless this doomed species also possessed midgets, was a giraffette. Plain as a stunted chimney.

Moreover, when it began moving again, it was obvious it was guiding me somewhere definite. We rattled over a bridge out of the wasteland and curled through more crooked thoroughfares into the absurdly-named Avenue Road. I anticipated yet another fatiguing pursuit down the middle of the street, but the beast stopped at one house and entered. It was Number 8, a structure with a squint. Most windows in Highgate look like eyes—the casements of this house needed spectacles.

Silently praising the owner who had left the door open, I followed. I stumbled in the myopic stairwell and crawled upward. My quarry was not far ahead, giggling quietly—I heard the creak of a rusty hinge. At the very top, a narrow corridor led to a door locked with acrid odours. This passage was almost as tall as a man who stands on tiptoe and has legs in place of arms. The giraffe had passed through the door—without pausing to wonder how, I turned the handle and pushed.

I found myself in a softly illuminated chamber, cluttered with all manner of arcane oddments. The giraffe stood facing me, a broad grin on its orange lips. Its posture was as menacing as the puppet of a spider. Coincidentally, I too mirrored a puppet—the shadow of an electrocuted marionette, limbs jerking in stringy rhythms.

Elusive Plato

Before engaging my prey, I took a lingering look at my surrounds. I was startled by the quantity of rare books and manuscripts on display, a rival to my father's study. Also I was gratified by the statues gracing the cobwebbed niches. Pallid busts of Adam Weishaupt, the arch-intriguer in wig and sneer, and of Basil Zaharoff, the cynical and successful arms dealer in pith helmet and beard, caught the satin lamplight. Both these gentlemen, as I have already stated, had dealings with my ancestors. It was certain that the owner of this chamber was a man after my own liver. I felt highly defensive of his property.

In the very centre of the scene, an impressive array of alchemical retorts and flasks simmered. An oven-like contrivance holding a pair of clear crystal eggs purred steadily in a network of conduits. My breasts prickled. This furnace, with its steaming coils and charred walls, the bowel-like tubes which strangled it, resembled a Cambrian growth that had refused to fossilise. When purple vapours spluttered from the flue, the effect was as sordid as a burning sea captain.

The giraffe pawed the carpet and I grew concerned for the delicate instruments, the jars of condensing wisdom. A host of these receptacles whistled the melody of my admonitions.

"Señor Giraffe, you have put up a brave resistance. But it has been more futile than bribing an angel. I do not wish to anoint this erudite room in your blood. Please come quietly."

This simple request met with an extraordinary response. The giraffe rippled in hideous mirth and replied:

"No, my pretty—'tis you who shall come to me. How I've toiled for this moment! Nigh on twenty years! And yet it seems but a single working day, for my life is a rabid coachman who whips the horses too hard. What more gorgeous virgin could I have found?"

I gagged on my own surprise. "A talking giraffe? But Papus Levi has nothing to say about this! I am alarmed."

"You've studied Levi?" The giraffe was delighted. "'Twill smooth the workings of my scheme! What is your name, fair maiden? I crave to become more acquainted in the old way before our bodies merge into the singular substance of the True Great Work!"

"The True Great Work? You mean the creation of a Hermaphrodite? A seamless blend of male and female elements?"

The giraffe stamped its hooves. "Yes, yes! At long last I have all the necessary ingredients. I have the rare powders and fluids, the lost tinctures of Ophir and Mu. I have read untranslated papyri from Assyria and Exeter. I have rowed through waterlogged archives in Venice, skated frozen libraries in Chaud-Mellé. I have spoken with the ghost of Corny Agrippa and shared crackers with the skeleton of Valentine Cheese. Even visited the gardens of Torrance-ap-Neith and picked pimplewort for the sleek complexion of my project."

"Surely not! You are a giraffe and would experience difficulties in turning the pages of untranslated papyri."

"As you please, my dear." The creature made another exquisite bow. "I do not wish to debate the matter."

I frowned. "I can accept the possibility of a verbose giraffe, one skilled in grammar and other aspects of linguistics, but the idea of an alchemical camelopard, proficient in the bubbling science, irks my most generous credulity. I am discomfited."

"That is of little consequence. Come, we must not linger. There is much work to do. You must cast off your brassière—twill only serve to interfere with the fusion. Hurry!"

This command was delivered with such confidence, I almost complied. I wondered if I had made an error in my classification of species. What if this was not a giraffe but an Æcuadoriac being, one of those demons herded in the Andes by Jesuit missionaries and given the name of llama? I seemed to recall that llamas were clever beggars and knew how to chant and pray. Yet they were supposed to be coloured saffron and this example had more of the turmeric about it.

Whatever it was, it started to grow impatient. "What's wrong? Don't you want to evolve? 'Tis most cowardly. It is within our power to finish God's uncompleted Creation. Salmacis!"

It stepped toward me and I levelled my pike. I knew the myth of the Fountain of Salmacis, the waters of which could congeal the two genders into an androgynous meta-genius, a rival to God. The synthesis of such waters was the aim of all alchemists. Needless to say, after recognising the threat, God had tried to make the necessary molecules unobtainable.

Was the quadruped really claiming success in this supreme quest? Was the stove gurgling before me, with its tubes of rushing liquids, a harnessed analogue of the forbidden Fountain?

"No-one is keener than I to assist the attainment of the True Great Work," I said, "but I am wary about giving over my body to a giraffe for such a purpose. Alchemy is for primates alone—when Papus Levi trained a mouse to stoke a furnace, his experiments and love affairs failed. He was forced to hire an orang-outang."

The giraffe ignored me. Like an earwig laureate, it waxed lyrical. "What care I about your reservations? Once I've sealed you in one ovoid crucible and melted your essence, I'll lower myself into the other. Our magmatic identities will blend and fill the mould of a living deity! We shall thumb our nose at the Holy Ghost!"

I studied the alchemical oven and saw that the crystal eggs drained into the cast of a two-headed figure. This was the real Hermaphrodite of legend; one part anima, one part animus, a dash of lemon. I doubted that a giraffe, even a small one, would fit in the receptacles. I voiced this opinion to my mottled interlocutor.

"Ha! You are virginal in sense as well as thigh." It quivered as if enduring an internal itch. "Twill be a pleasure sharing your soul. Don't judge by appearances, my dear. I'm bipedal."

I heaved an enormous sigh. My patience had ground to flour; my fury trampled all over it, kicking up inflammatory clouds. I weighed the pike more comfortably in my burning palms.

"Señor Giraffe, I detect trickery in your speech. I deem this talk a ruse to distract my attention. Alchemy is too complex a science to be mastered by an animal without hands. I suggest you have picked up a few keywords and are seeking to delude me with them. Besides, this room does not seem the abode of a savannah dweller."

"But it is! And I am the new Adam looking for a wife. You'll be my Lilith! Kiss my slobbery lips, my darling!"

I scowled and thrust with my pike. No giraffe was going to petition me for a smooch while I bore the Cadiz name—conjoining with foxes and crows and moles was one thing. My lunge caught the beast in the sternum. There was a hiss of escaping air and the quadruped deflated. The weapon recoiled into my navel as two hands appeared from inside the rent. They gripped the edges of the wound and wrenched it open. The ruddy shell of the disguise fell away in two pieces.

"A fabric camelopard!" I wailed. Remembering my previous utterance in the office, while hiding from the lions, I amended it: "Oh, Bartleby! You are not so eligible now! How fortunate you did not accept my offer of marriage. I would seek a divorce."

The man who occupied the place of the giraffe brushed himself down and adjusted his round glasses. He owned the type of face and form that is condemned always to be sheathed in tweed. He rummaged in a pocket and took out a packet of absinthe-soaked phëresli, rolling a cigarette with chubby but dexterous fingers. Hunching over one of the flames sprouting from his apparatus, he puffed contentedly.

"I chanced my neck and was rewarded handsomely! Such a fine virgin from among a whole squeal of 'em! What better soul mate could I ask for? Twill be ample compensation for my efforts."

I teetered and embraced a statue for support. This was yet another visage I recognised—before me, exhaling smoke like phantom worms, was the occult savant my mother had written to all those years before. From the signed photograph he had enclosed, I was familiar with his guileful eyes and archaic fringe. He smoked his papelito down to the tips of his yellow fingers and flicked the stub aside.

"Of course, when I'm androgynous, my identity subsumed into that of the sacred Hermaphrodite, I won't need nicotine. Twill be a release from mundane habits as well as a deification."

"But why such an elaborate stratagem to obtain a virgin? There is a town on the edge of London where they can be hired. I forget the name of it. Papus Levi resided there for a year."

Rolling another cigarette, this time full of pernod-soaked sativa, the alchemist snorted. "You mean Maidenhead? 'Tis no longer appropriate for my needs. Settlers from Staines have punctured the artificial hymen which covered it. Already it is pregnant with another suburb. No, I had to be sure of my source. For an Usher, the purity rules are fixed. Only Guild Members are as indubitably unused as my own member!" Lowering his voice to the level of his bulging loins, he winked. "Oh, yes. I've been saving myself for this enterprise."

"In that case, why adopt the appearance of a giraffe? Would not hog or horse have been less ponderous?"

"You dare to suggest I dress myself up as a pig! You are remarkably forward for an uninfected girl. 'Tis a housewife's banter! But I have a soft spot for bawdy virgins. Would you like to see it?" Before I had the chance to demur at his offer, he undid his belt and dropped his trousers to the floor, forming two puddles of rough woollen cloth over his highly polished shoes. My gaze was spitted on the result.

Elusive Plato

Like my father, he obviously deemed underpants a needless sartorial extravagance. But it was some moments before I realised this—his flesh was the colour and texture of tweed, scarcely different from that of his suit. I reckoned it to be a slightly more costly weave. His member, only skilled in the theoretical aspects of carnal love, stood less proud than haughty. I began to retch on the pattern.

His own pike, more lethal than mine in bedroom sieges, flexed twice as he stepped forward. He removed his glasses, wiped them on his manroot and replaced them. "Now I see you better! Overlooking the beard, you are as ravishing as Salmacis herself. She too was a virgin when she combined with Hermaphroditus, son of Quicksilver and the first Venus. God will be kicking himself with his club foot!"

"I caution restraint. Although I have never bedded a man, I am not what I seem. Indeed, my chromosomes may upset the delicate manipulation of the True Great Work. Much better to seek another Usher. I have massy influence in the Guild; I will aid you."

For the first time, the alchemist's laugh seemed unforced. "Callow ploys won't help you. I have everything I need. Twill be churlish not to proceed on this basis. Come hither, lusty!"

The militant blood of my forefathers erupted in my arteries. Beside my kidneys, my adrenal glands stamped their feet. My neck bulged with an awful pressure. I aimed my pike at the savant's lingam, marching forward in a grisly shuffle. I cried righteously:

"Enough of this cabbalism! My duty is to protect not only my virtue but that of my sisters. Look to your organ!"

Faster than a hen, the alchemist jumped the crystal eggs and landed by a shelf filled with strange jars. Some were tagged with various kinds of dream; others with more likely substances. He snatched an example of chloroform and threw it in a careful arc at my feet.

As it exploded, and the limpid vapours engulfed me, I was aware of him posturing wildly. He was acting his whole life story—he did not realise it was my biography which was supposed to be passing in front of my drowning consciousness. In some ways, this substitute pantomime was more interesting; in others, it aided the soporiferousness of his assault.

The alchemist was called Mark Xeethra Samuels and was yet another exile from the Alpine republic. He knew both the midget artisan and Reverend Douglas Delves—though not passionately. Delves had once been a member of his secret society. There was trouble with Austria, some sort of war, and the republic was reduced to shards. He was vague about the details.

Unlike other members of the Cadiz dynasty, I was not greatly interested in the game of international politics. I did not press him to elaborate. Of greater concern was my immediate fate. On this he was most eloquent, outlining every detail of his intentions.

The chloroform wore off within an hour. My mind re-entered my brain like a dismissed valet applying for the position of a maid. During these confusing minutes, I was dreamily aware of the alchemist's rough fingers rummaging under my brassière. His squint was as extended as when he had sported his disguise—I flapped helplessly under him, a bird with wings disqualified by God.

He was conducting a medical examination; to create the mystical Hermaphrodite, rather than one of those prosaic mutants who share the same label, it is essential that both components of the deity are utterly pure. Else the matrix will not set.

He did not move me to a more comfortable location, but manipulated my parts on the uneven floor. He used a slide-rule to measure the depth of my dimples, the coyness of my nose; he pulled my nipples to estimate their tensile strength. He was satisfied with the result.

Finally, down between my legs he delved, noting the features of my vagina's geography, then descending into its geology, discovering to his horror that the pit had already been opened for exploitation.

The tattered edges of my broken hymen fluttered in the flavours of his breath. "What's this? A fake virgin? But the Ushers are strict! 'Tis a wondrous anomaly and one worthy of reporting to the Guild. You will be condemned to brusque tortures for this act of impiety. Twill make a good subject for my latest academic paper."

I was relieved to have escaped his attentions so easily. I tried to speak, to amplify his doubts, but the chemical had parched my voice into quietude. So I nodded as vigorously as my debilitated neck muscles would allow. He studied this gesture thoughtfully.

"What are you trying to tell me? 'Tis surely of some great urgency. Oscillating your head thus! What does it signify? Ah, I have it! You are indicating a seesaw! You perforated your hymen in an acceptable way. I'm soothed by this news; it redeems you."

Cutting free the shreds of hymen with a scalpel and arranging them on a glass slide, he placed the partly reconstructed maidenhead under a microscope and adjusted the focus. "There's writing here!" he squealed. "Much of the text is missing, but I might be able to decipher the rest. Po Jo, hom ina, Co Sten? This makes no sense at all! Wait, what's this? Virgin Wool! Ah, must be a trademark."

A groan escaped my lips. My best chance, however, had not yet come. When he finished with his microscope, he returned to my fallopian tubes. After a wary forage, like a pessimist trying a lucky dip, he chanced on the severed hand and gin-trap. Pulling out both, he regarded them with a face creased diagonally with repugnance. The Captain's flesh had started to decay; his thumb was a tazelwurm.

Encrusted in sub-vaginal deposits, the palm glistened in the rusty jaws like a leprous octopus caught by an emaciated clam. Disappointment once more ironed flat the savant's tweedy member. Thoughts of my release loomed in his eyes sunken galleon style.

Again I tried to consolidate my position. "Captain Nothing!" I said aloud, but only the first letter sputtered from my lips. I repeated this name, to the same effect. Too exhausted to make a third attempt, I could do nothing but fall back and gnash the echo.

The alchemist rolled the stuttered letters in his ear, snapping his fingers. "Cervical cancer! Tumours occasionally look like hands or feet. This oncological growth even has a ring on its second finger. 'Tis lucky I removed it before it developed an arm."

I knew he was determined to have me as his virgin, whatever oddity he discovered. Even were he to know of my true nature, he would probably concoct an elaborate excuse to account for it, attributing my misplaced masculinity to the effects of malaria of some other Iberian disease and my sapphism to the overindulgence of figs.

I therefore did not protest when he carried me over to the furnace and opened the side of a crystal egg. He bundled me inside—

where I had to adopt a foetal position—and locked the piece of arcane apparatus. I was now the yolk of the same philosophy my mother had struggled to crack into the saucepan of her ambition. How envious she would be of my ovoid plight! She would dribble albumen in excitement if she but knew! Ironies hatch everywhere in our poached existence.

Fully removing his clothes, Mark Xeethra Samuels prepared to climb into the other receptacle. He was interrupted by a knock on the door. I prayed it was a colleague come to rescue me. The Personnel Officer bore tender feelings for me, I knew. Perhaps she had secretly followed me in the hope of wooing me a second time?

I pounded against the smooth walls of my crystal prison; they were as unyielding as jars of green ink. The cramp which gripped my legs was unbearable—the air inside the egg was as stale as that of a publisher's breath.

The alchemist opened the door carelessly, though he was still nude. The woman who stood on the threshold offered him no more than a cursory glance. She carried a mop and bucket and her flaxen hair was bound up in complicated spirals. She took a spacious rag from a pocket and proceeded to dust the statues and occult paraphernalia.

Sighing, the alchemist said, "Late again, Dotty. 'Tis not polite to disturb a gentleman in the middle of a quasi-miracle. Be quick with your work; I have urgent meldings to attend!"

She bowed and coughed. "Véry göod, Màstër Sâmuéls. Päy extrà ând I gö nòw, no fûss. Whát yöu sày, féllöw?"

I frowned. The hussy obviously suffered from a speech impediment. I was tempted to admire the alchemist for trying to converse with her. But then it struck me that he was a callous opportunist, willing to entice a virgin away from a *venatione* by dressing up as a giraffe. So my sympathy evaporated as rapidly as my hope. I tried to attract the hag's attention with a frantic wave, but she ignored me.

With outrageous ineptitude, she continued her menial task, circling the chamber, cleaning the retorts and alembics. Stoically, Mark Xeethra Samuels took refuge in a rocking chair.

Majestically, he smoked twelve different cheroots in a contraption designed for the parallel chain smoker.

Eventually, the hussy approached the oven and polished my

oubliette from the outside. By this time, I had regained my voice. My words burst through the hermetic seal:

"Your master lured me here to corrupt my body and soul. What do you think of that? Run to fetch help!"

"Nò büsinêss óf minë if hè énjöy bit öf cörrúptiòn."

I fumed. "What is the matter with her? I know that people who clean for a living are devoid of pity for Spaniards, but they generally manage to express their loathing coherently."

The alchemist exhaled a multi-coloured nimbus. "She's from Cologne. In her home town, her phrases are tinged with perfume. 'Tis how the city earned its name. Unfortunately, such odours translate badly. In English, it sounds as if she is placing inappropriate accents on vowels. Her name is Dotty Umlaut. She's harmless enough."

I tried again: "Do you wish to become an accessory to heresy? What will God think of you if you allow your master to set himself up as some sort of rival? He will smite your mops!"

Mark Xeethra Samuels sniggered. "She's not a Nazarene. The burghers of Cologne still worship Woden. 'Tis why I hired her. Christian cleaners would scrub the blasphemy from my chamber."

Dotty made a curtsy even more unstable than my own. "I kèëp háving thêsé strängè ürgês. Invädè änd sáck Römê."

I was horrified. "Sack Rome? But the redundancy settlement would be crippling. I think it appropriate to warn you that despite my absolutely evil personality, I am a loyal supporter of the Vatican and will do what I can to preserve its reputation and décor."

My finest sentiments had no impact on her flaxen conscience. Whilst the savant lounged with a book, the servant spat on her rag and used her corrosive saliva to dissolve all grime.

I was surprised to note that the alchemist was perusing the memoirs of Caligula and that the tome was open on the page where the narrator is appalled by the antics of my ancestors.

With as much attentiveness as a necklace, Dotty Umlaut scoured the crystal eggs until the sparkle singed my lashes. She completed the stove with a stiff-armed salute and opened an adjoining door into another room of the apartment. I glimpsed a viler set of exhibits; rows of very large flasks holding the pickled bodies of waxen women. In amontillado vinegar they swirled, unknowingly rapping on the glass with balsamic knuckles, sightless eyes smarting from the dressing.

Mark Xeethra Samuels gestured through the door. "'Tis where I keep my failures. Each year, I've tried to capture a virgin. Even though the alchemical recipe wasn't ready, I thought it wise to stock up. But they were never pure! I could hardly return them back to the ordinary world, where they might alert the authorities and disrupt my work. So I bought vinegar and renewed their salad days!"

I nodded. "Very generous. But I recognise that fellow. He tried to threaten me on the road from Dover."

One of the pickled figures was plainly male and still alive. Under a crumpled tricorne hat, a folklorish face grimaced. Black teeth shone like obsidian altars. A locket tied around his throat, sealed with some material lighter than amontillado vinegar, bobbed at the top of the jar, tightening the chain and making him look like a hung rascal. His pupils contained decades of disappointment.

The alchemist puffed his cheeks. "'Tis my highwayman. I caught him just before I enticed you. I donned my giraffe outfit and waited in the shadows for an Usher. Suddenly, the barrel of a wheel-lock pistol jabbed the nape of my neck. The fool was holding me up! I protested that I was a giraffe. It made no difference. I ran and he chased me here. 'Tis why I was so late returning to the *venatione*. Thought I'd missed my chance! Happily, you were lagging far behind."

I struck my brow. Had I not tried to cheat, I would not now be in this ludicrous position. I hate episodes with morals—they have never been favourable among the Cadiz family.

"There is something peculiar about him," I ventured. "How does he manage to breathe without air? His constitution must be unique. And his gums are more inflamed than bubonic eunuchs in a putrefying harem. What mortal could bear such poor quality pearlies?"

Mark Xeethra Samuels agreed. "I suspect he is neither man nor myth but an amalgam of the two. In some ways, he will make a perfect witness to our fusion—it may not be dissimilar to his own. I mean the process rather than the result. Perhaps I shall wheel him next to the oven when the time is right." He consulted his pocket watch, a showy Alpine model in the shape of a miniature clock tower. "Hurry up, Dotty! I'm growing impatient to become a new kind of god!"

"Yöú wânt thé jòb döné pröpèrly, Màstër Sâmuéls?"

Elusive Plato

It was impossible to proceed with the True Great Work before the alchemist's cleaner had finished. I gazed with rapturous misery at the preserved highwayman; he winked at me and I blushed. Dotty Umlaut, for her part, was in no rush—she was as thorough as a saw. Once more the pickled unfortunate opened and closed his eye. How dare he flirt with a Guild virgin? I protested to the alchemist.

"'Tis how he communicates," Mark Xeethra Samuels avowed. "No sooner had I sealed him in the jar than he struck up a conversation. He claimed to have been an alchemist also; he mistreated the science, calling it an art, and it punished him in some unspecified way. I believe it compelled him to hold perverse notions. Each flap of an eyelid stands for a letter of the Saracen language, as delineated by Sir John Mandeville. They are pronounced as follows: almoy, bethath, cathi . . . "

"Intriguing. But my name is Bartleby Cadiz, which in the philology of mercy means, 'One Who Has Heard Enough'."

Mark Xeethra Samuels shrugged. "Twill be better not to continue. My learning is ordered alphabetically. I have not yet reached etymology. I started at the beginning of the dictionary and am working my way through the subjects. I am the ultimate authority on aardvarks and agoraphobia. When I've finished with alchemy, I'll start on alcohol and algebra. With your half's permission, of course."

"What do you know of love?"

"Very little. I briefly touched on Agape—the love of God for man. But it didn't return the favour. I know that a virgin placed at an equal distance between erotic and spiritual love will die of loneliness, being unable to choose between the two . . . "

"Have you heard of a third kind of love? Platonic love?" My breath steamed my prison. I wiped a spy hole.

Mark Xeethra Samuels rolled a large reefer of mastika-soaked nutmeg and made an Oriental kitchen of his chamber. Soon my hermetic egg was a bubble of clarity in a smoky universe. His reply was like the prow of a longboat approaching the Orkneys—his integrity was shielded down both sides of his carved personality.

"Plato, you say? 'Tis an abstruse topic for a virgin to express an interest in. Do you perform fellatio?"

"Never. Like yourself, I am a scholar. This is why you must not use me in your experiment. It will endanger my own researches. I am questing for a third alternative to Agape and Eros—a love which owes nothing to either but lies somewhere in the middle."

The alchemist became agitated. He finished his cigarette and made a few radical adjustments to his fringe.

"Curiosity killed the Herodotus! Twill never be safe to delve into matters of such complexity. Even when we mingle and overthrow God, 'tis doubtful we'll be able to alter the geometrical laws of space, time and sex. Platonic love is logically contradictory!"

Before I could question him further on this statement, the prickly tones of Dotty Umlaut thrust from an adjacent cell: "Màstër Sâmuéls, hê knów äll àböút thät dirty òld Athënián."

The alchemist raised his fists. "Silence, Dotty! I've not forgiven you for turning my telescope into a cannon and firing me over the roofs of London!" He turned to me and cleared his throat. "Ignore her. A fever of the imagination caused by proximity to detergent. Despite her claims, I'm unfamiliar with Plato's message."

I shifted in my crystal womb. "I will decode it."

He lowered his voice and tapped his nose. "Twill not be easy. Once part of me, I'll forbid you to try. The works—and woks—of Plato are best left in the dusty larder of paradox."

I mulled the problem as my oxygen thinned. Though willing to accept that Platonic love had no place in my world, this did not mean the basic concept was invalid. What if it existed on a different plane, in another dimension, parallel to this one?

The idea of simultaneous realities had previously held little appeal for me—I deemed it a conceit of scholars bored or bullied by their wives. But the schema of this vision was clear and alluring—it had to thrive somewhere. Perhaps in a universe unknown to God or one which rejected His rule?

My fancies were goaded by Dotty, who had sharpened her clusters of inappropriate accents until they resembled Ushers' pikes. Emerging from the room of pickles, she climbed inside a dumb waiter connecting a deep basement with the chamber. Her rag fluttered like a pie. "Always tëlling úntrûths àböút pöör Dötty is Màstër Sâmuéls, hârdly fáir. If hë hás nöt réâd Hërr Plátô, thën why hé plày thë Xénöphònê in thé èvënings? Tinklè, tinklè âll night; I knöw. Alsó I clëán his bööks."

At this, the alchemist lost his temper. He snatched up a flask from the shelf behind the stove and hurled it against the hatch of the dumb waiter. It cracked; a cloud of purple mist spiraled toward the ceiling. Like a septic djinn, it turned yellow and folded in half. In the stomach of the fog, a man played an antique piano.

"Father!" I cried. The Bösendorfer expanded and dissipated, cut to ribbons by the fanning of the alchemist's tweed handkerchief. "Where did this mirage originate? My pater is dead!"

Mark Xeethra Samuels nodded sombrely. "Another of my hobbies is the collecting of dreams. While you were incapacitated by the chloroform, my fingers stole your favourite memory." He indicated the ranks of bottles. "It's lost now; you're an archetype short."

"I dispute this. My father never used his thumbs in my presence. It is a scene unrelated to my psychology."

"The dream was not entirely yours. When we sleep, our fantasies run away from home and look for a job. If successful, they invite workmates back for supper. 'Tis not unknown for a man to have upwards of a hundred outside dreams cluttering up his mind."

"My favourite memory did not belong to me?"

The alchemist rubbed his palms. "I suspect it was one owned by your father which took up permanent residence in your brain. 'Tis always this way. It showed you something you'd never seen."

I was forced to acknowledge his wisdom. My father pounding the keys of the piano had always been a source of great comfort and despair. Long ages I had yearned to watch him play with his thumbs. The alchemist made a note of my interest and confessed to having filched a dream from every person he had come into contact with.

"You are as unscrupulous as a tricycle," I observed. "But we wander from the subject. Your cleaner hints you have volumes on Plato. Before I melt into the True Great Work, I demand a final request. Show me all you possess concerning him. What was his surname?"

From the interior of the dumb-waiter, Dotty Umlaut piped up: "Thát sö̈und rèâsö̈náblè tö̈ mê, Màstër Sâmuéls. Knóck hèr ä mêlódy ön yóür bôny Xénöphònê. Undêr thè bëd, it résidës!"

The savant managed to control his passion. "Dotty, always you harry me. 'Tis not a Xenophone but a Glockenspengler. The former sounds chords like milking a goat; the second prefers declining western arpeggios. But neither instrument was invented by Plato! He limited himself to saucers, dishes and speculations. 'Tis certain."

I frowned and tried to deduce the relevance of such arcane musical devices to my tuneless search. Mark Xeethra Samuels enlightened me with diminishing reluctance. He had decided, he announced, to be as frank as I desired; not because it was the proper thing to do, but because there should be no hard feelings between two parts of a divine Hermaphrodite. We would, after all, be inseparable for the remainder of our marvellous lives.

I thanked him for his compassion and in return promised to take the left side of the True Great Work without rancour—he was unable to accomplish anything with his sinistral edge.

The Xenophone, he explained, was an ancient type of marimba, struck with mallets and popular among classical sophists. They were constructed according to hidden directions in the poems of Sappho. At this name, my nipples solidified.

The alchemist disregarded my mounting excitement and went on to deny any relationship between the instrument and the obscure potter known as Plato, save that they were contemporaneous. Dotty Umlaut was inclined to associate dissimilar entities; it was probably a sign of mental illness. He would have deposited her in a madhouse years ago were she not such a comprehensive scrubber.

My attention was distracted by a very subtle hiss from the deeps of a niche. I saw nothing but my unease was exacerbated. The savant treated it as dismissively as a pygmy's dandruff.

"I do have works which mention Plato," he admitted. "'Tis unlikely they tell the truth. Hard facts are as scarce as carnivorous lambs; the medieval thaumaturge, Raymond Lullaby, recounts that Plato resided in a dank cavern and conjoined with stalagmites."

"I have heard something similar. A troglodyte."

"The manuscripts which mention him are too shy to be read aloud. My own collection does not like to be handled more than once a month. Twill annoy it immensely to be discussed in public. 'Tis immoral to read books anyhow—they are made from the flesh of trees. In future ages, we shall be regarded as Scythian in our barbarity!"

"But God has ordained plants as the servants of animals. Less cruel to make books than the oars of galleys!"

"Once the True Great Work is completed, the coming order of society will be unpredictable. God's script will no longer apply; the human race must needs write its own. Cruelty shall be redefined. I envisage empathy with vegetation and nastiness to minerals!"

Elusive Plato

I bit my lip and said nothing. As half of the divine Hermaphrodite, I would do my utmost to water down his reforms—with beer if need be. I shrugged in my receptacle. I estimated I had another twelve arguments in total before my air expired.

It seemed obvious that Plato had discovered something unknown to God: a new way of regarding fellow citizens. Unable to completely suppress his ideas, the deity had forced them to adopt odd forms.

At that moment, I felt an ineffable sympathy for Yahweh—men and women were always challenging Him, constipating His eschatology, combing the slimy fringe of His authority, shaving His toothbrush moustache with Occam's razor. Humanity was mimicking Heaven, like a governess who seeks to rouge her nipples to housewife standards.

"'Tis impossible to separate truth from untruth," added the savant. "The little that has been written does not concur. 'Tis not even certain what Plato's favourite food was. One source says lettuce; another claims emeralds. The quality of his pots is also indeterminate. Raymond Lullaby suggested his plates were arrogant saucers."

I scratched my chin. "I would like to read the text of one of these tomes. Are they all too coy to be opened in my presence? I will use only my right eye, if it will spare their blushes."

Mark Xeethra Samuels prowled to one of his bookshelves and caressed the spine of an octavo. "I believe the genuine accounts to be as winsome as a Japanese seamstress; the forgeries are more forward. That maverick, Valentine Cheese, was responsible for many of the counterfeits. Consider this fraudulent classic . . . " He pulled a warped folio, more sly than shy, from its resting place and waved it aloft.

I recognised the notoriously mouldy *Gruyère of Honorious*, which had fooled students all over the continent. This forgery had been the source of innumerable failed experiments and bank accounts. An edition bound in paraffin wax had been printed by a Tartarean press in Horam a month before my leaving. Valentine Cheese, bless his cholesterol socks, was a man whose conscience had no rind. And yet all this was tangential to the wisdom I sought. I berated the alchemist for lingering on subjects which marginalised my concerns. "Plato!" I cried.

Still inside the dumb waiter, Dotty echoed my plea: "Tréât him wíth cöntèmpt, Fräû Háiry. Hè knöws àll thë fácts."

Mark Xeethra Samuels sighed. "I might as well reveal the sum. Twill not satisfy you, but could unburden my soul. That dirty old Athenian, as Dotty terms him, is as elusive as an Arimaspi. I've cobbled together ten reliable details by cutting a fact from each account. Cross referencing, like cross dressing, has enabled me to garter the stocking of doubt. Now I have a seamed version of Plato's biography."

"So what are the fundaments of his love?"

"Hazardous to contemplate. It seems he went mad after being kissed by a man with hemlock flavoured lips. The event persuaded him to reject erotic love, but he was unable to immerse himself in spiritual lust. He placed the clay of emotion on his potter's wheel and span a new one: he gave it the anfractuous name of 'Friendship'."

"This teaches me nothing. Jargon is for obfuscationists. How would one apply Platonic love to a burning virgin? The present options are to smother with gropes or bless with gripes."

"There is neither a priapic nor seraphic release."

"What then? Quick; I am ablaze myself!"

"It seems to mean feeling affection for someone without wishing to impregnate their bodies or spirits. 'Tis not entirely altruistic; nor as selfish as it should be. There is no sperm involved and few prayers are muttered. 'Tis extremely difficult to imagine. Like trying to picture a microscopic giant. A Platonist might extinguish a burning virgin simply to help ensure a return of the favour. Yet even this is not an essential principle. The mathematical formulae for this love are not forthcoming. 'Tis peripheral to our mode of reality."

I nodded. "I am more convinced than before that it is intended for a separate dimension. Somehow Plato hooked it and tried to reel it into our world. But the task was too much for him."

The alchemist wiped his mouth with his handkerchief. "Doubtless you are correct. 'Tis why I'm loathe to investigate further. I wish to probe every subject of this cosmos before disrobing alternate realities. Greed will be our undoing; let's embrace one set of arcana at a time. The True Great Work has priority over multiversifying."

"But meditate the consequences! In our universe, God's

existence is indubitable, but 'friendship' is an unconfirmed abstraction. Might there be some cosmos where the opposite is the case? A reality where no-one is sure of the actuality of the Divinity, but where Plato's weird affection is established. What would such a place be like?"

"These games will drive me to raging insanity! But I'll humour you. The dimension you postulate would be superficially similar to our own; a few glaring differences would permeate the fabric of society. 'Tis silly to say, but I suspect your hypothetical world to be one where housewives float like other women and their nipples don't resemble noses; where the realm is unified and there are less wars— though not a great many less; where disappointment is tasted with the upper lip rather than the lower; where London has a system of underground trains; where cucumbers contain iron, or other metals, rather than sunlight."

"Now you have ventured beyond my wildest speculations. Such a place could never connect with our own."

"Oh, I dare say a gateway might be opened up. In geometry there's a mandala-like shape known a tesseract . . . "

Before the alchemist could continue, Dotty Umlaut leaned out of the dumb-waiter's insides and folded her rag. "Finïshéd nòw, Màstër Sâmuéls. Yóu mây pùt thé chärgê òn yöúr âccòünt."

"No, Dotty. I'll pay in full now; I have no more use for you. When I'm divine, I won't require a cleaner."

The hag visibly stiffened. "On thè cöntráry, göds átträct dûst lìkê chëésêmòngérs. Bèst kêëp mé ön, bóss-màn."

"'Tis a fretful notion, my dear. I'm afraid I have to let you go. I shall throw in a bratwurst as a bonus."

With a furious glower, Dotty Umlaut folded her arms and adopted the lotus position in the middle of the dumb waiter. I was obliged to wonder aloud why she had spent such a long time on that one machine, while the swabbing of the intricate retorts and flasks had taken her the lifespan of a bite. Mark Xeethra Samuels explained that the device shuttled acids from his cellar to his laboratory and that the spilt liquids could only be neutralised by Dotty's alkaline mucus.

"'Twill be the last time her drool is set to work on my possessions. Gods are sparkling; we'll eradicate stains with our brains. Come, Dotty, be reasonable. 'Tis an unteutonic huff."

"Nô, Màstër Sâmuéls, yóu trêàt më tóô crùël."

Steeping forward casually, the alchemist depressed a lever set into the wall and the dumb waiter plummeted down, taking the cleaner with it. So rapid and unexpected was her fall that only the jagged accents of her vowels, rather than the actual letters, remained on her scream. Right at the nadir of the descent lay a terrific crash; Dotty and sound met in an orgy of implosive fury. The alchemist chuckled.

Opening a cupboard, he removed a sausage from a hook and dropped it after her. "I always keep my promises," he said. The stench of bratwurst reminded me of my Brighton lodgings. But the immediacy of my plight soon replaced this reverie, assaulting it with clubs whittled from the shafts of spades. My individualism was bankrupt.

"Please do not turn me into an Hermaphrodite," I pleaded. "My legs are too reclusive to socialise."

"There's a saying in Chaud-Mellé—never mind the gâteau, feel the thigh. 'Tis a spongy enough maxim."

Mark Xeethra Samuels turned up the flame of the stove and unlocked the second crystal egg. Then he squeezed within and slammed it shut. No way out now, other than through the tubes which mixed our melted beings and deposited the alloy into the double-headed mould.

Already my facial muscles were dripping down my chin. Along the conduits, the voice of my imminent other half vibrated like a pensioner in a cyclone. Crusty skin bubbled and oozed; my nose detached itself and began wriggling down the inside wall of my prison. The salted slugs of my fingers followed, in a pathetic attempt to peel it off and reunite it with my gaping olfactory inlets. I wrestled with panic and was thrown.

Wriggling to cool my torso, I yapped like a tide in the dog days. A snake, hooded and sultry, slithered from behind a statue and reared high before the stove—the source of the earlier hiss.

Despite the thickness of crystal which separated us, I instinctively recoiled and hunched both shoulders. Its venomous lips were like two halves of an open purse. So I bellowed at my host in a tumescent voice, as if my neck had already been punctured. "A cobra is watching me!"

"'Tis merely Florence. She's my favourite pet. Found her underneath the crust of one of Kipling's cakes."

Elusive Plato

This was an extra complication. Even if a miracle occurred and the hermetic egg shattered, I would not be able to escape easily. The choice between fang and flame did not reassure.

The alchemist preserved a scientific detachment throughout most of the ordeal. "Another thing about your imagined dimension," he observed, as the eggs started to glow, "is that its citizens possibly do not melt as we do, at specific temperatures. Pure conjecture, of course, but one based on sweet intuitive analytics."

I scrabbled to escape the pervading inferno. My feet pushed against the quartz curve. I tumbled and span within the womb. While my tormentor babbled objective theories on seventeen subjects at once, I succeeded in reversing my foetal posture. My skull now rested on the crucible's base. Inverted, I regarded my environs with antipodean sorrow. Now I was truly stuck, unable to move in any direction.

Mark Xeethra Samuels noted my predicament and wailed in alarm. "How did you get upside-down? Return to your original discomfort immediately! Twill upset the balance of the amalgamation."

I attempted to comply with his request, but my flesh was turning to liquid. The bottom of my prison swirled with my essence; it gurgled down the plughole and along the glass tubes.

"I am unable to seek purchase on the smooth walls. My feet are too runny to afford secure grip. Adios, amoeba!"

"Imbecile! You've ruined the True Great Work!"

My eyes dribbled from their sockets, floating on the surface of the rapidly draining fluid. Still connected to their optic nerves, they were able to gauge the situation from a new perspective.

The alchemist was in a molten state also. I saw his fringe dissolve and the tweed patterns of his skin unravel. His member resembled a candle used by an undergraduate the night prior to an examination. It gutted and broiled. His guts broke loose from his disintegrating abdomen and thrashed in the stock. We were sucked down and blended in a single pipe, pouring into the mould of that paradisal parasite, the elysian Hermaphrodite.

Drowning in my own puréed corporality, I was aware of the pet snake undulating in time to my screams. Then my vocal abilities were curtailed as my entire palate turned to a crimson mush. My senses withdrew support from the body's cause, retiring to unknown corners of unawareness.

I did not feel pain as I was drawn into the tight spiral of rushing ichor. All that remained was the faintest tinge of cognizance. Cast by a niche-lamp hung over a bust of Count Joseph de Gobineau, the shadow of the alembics warbled on an uneven wall. It seemed I was peering not at a penumbra but through a thinning wall into a chamber existing in a parallel dimension, a room different from ours in two essential details.

Last to go, my eyes followed my head, body and limbs; then the molecules of my identity were binding with those of Mark Xeethra Samuels.

I reawakened to consciousness subtly, like a congealing jelly. With a fructuous groan, I mentally figured the angles of my form. The cosines of my navel and armpits had altered their sweaty values. A bulge annoyed my groin; the alchemist was not on my right side, his reserved place.

We had not blended in the anticipated fashion. Breathing lightly, with four lungs, I levered myself out of the mould, that sacrilegious sarcophagus. The empty eggs above reflected my noisomeness.

For a moment, I could not grasp the nature of the failure. Instead of possessing two heads and four arms, my own head was the sole flag on the summit of the alpine androgyne. But two flapping legs protruded from my shoulders. My gait was awkward, as if I was once more the proud owner of a set of testicles, hideously bloated. Where was the alchemist? What had happened to his designated half?

I rubbed my groin and received an answer from below: "Careful! Mind your grubby fingers in my eyes! Idiot!"

Glancing down, I beheld the savant's head wedged between my thighs. His mouth occupied the place of my vagina. Once more, I was armed with a set of nether-teeth. "What are you doing in my main erogenous zone? This is aggravated trespass! Avaunt at once!"

"You utter fool! 'Tis a catastrophe!"

I frowned and staggered across the chamber into a chair. I found it impossible to sit down in the correct manner; the alchemist's skull made it advisable to perch on the very edge.

"How did we arrive at such an unpretty pass?" I inquired. My vagina was hardly reticent; it railed against me for an hour before pausing for breath. Being insulted by one's own sex is a novel experience; hitherto, only magazine editors and draughtspersons risked this singular hazard. I waited for it to finish and picked its gums with my fingers. This action made it dribble and contract in powerful waves.

"Profanity!" it groaned. "The matrix has not set. The Hermaphrodite isn't a seamless blend! 'Twill be the end of us! What protection from God will this abominable shape provide?"

By rotating in the hermetic crucible and melting while upside-down, I was solely responsible for the resultant monster. Mark Xeethra Samuels and Bartleby Cadiz should have been superimposed upon each other. But my body blended at the wrong angle, a complete half turn, and we were fused in this absurd and ignominious position. Erect, I was condemned to carry the inverted alchemist inside me, his head forcing my thighs apart, arms branching from my hips.

I poked my tongue and realised to my horror that it was his flaccid manroot, incapable of tasting anything but salt. Each lick of a spoon would be a rape of a concavity. I trembled at visions of my future life, a swivelled Siamese twin.

Interestingly, Mark Xeethra Samuels regarded me as the inverted one and himself as entitled to stand on his feet whilst I dangled within. It was a curious way of looking at the situation. I disputed his assertions with a penile eloquence, though he struggled to warp my words by flexing his member. "Be content with your status!" I ejaculated, in both senses. "No Cadizite has ever walked on his hands!"

"You Spanish minx! The blood is rushing to my head. I'll die if you don't put me the right way up. Please!"

"Do it yourself, you exploiter."

Seizing the legs of the chair, his arms pulled it down and threw me to the floor. Then his own legs bent at the knee and he sprang up, while I was turned over and hung like a grouse from the beams of his skeleton. He giggled and inserted a cigarette into my vagina—his mouth—and lit it by leaning over the loathsome stove.

"'Tis only fair. You wrecked the experiment, not I."

"Might we re-melt ourselves and claim back our original forms? Why not alter the apparatus to achieve this?"

"Impossible! Our molecules are inextricably linked! The alchemical valency which holds them together can't be broken without all the atoms coming apart. 'Tis an irreversible blunder!"

I sobbed. Forever doomed to share a single structure with a

tweedy fellow! He bent to wipe my nose and my arms grabbed his knees, shifting his balance. Now my legs, projecting from his collar bones, kicked at a statue of Baron von Ungern-Sternberg and we tumbled a second time. Once more, it was my turn to gain ascendancy. I pulled the cigarette from my vagina and stubbed it on the savant's forehead. "No Benedictine-soaked opium in my mary!" I cried. "It is unhygenic!"

Mark Xeethra Samuels howled with humiliation. His fists pounded on my stomach. I decided to smother him, plugging my sex with one of Dotty Umlaut's abandoned rags and pinching his nostrils.

My murder attempt had an unforeseen result. As he began to asphyxiate, his member expanded and blocked my throat. I also began to choke. It seemed I could not cut off his oxygen supply without endangering my own.

So I released my grip and collapsed in a daze, waiting for his lethal erection to subside. A hardy spirit, he recovered first and used my physical weakness to reverse our relative positions for a third time . . .

Thus began an evening of unlikely gymnastics. We swapped situations whenever we had a chance, cartwheeling around the chamber, knocking into alembics and telescopes and bookshelves.

Mostly, when we fell, the stronger one at that moment would compel the other to mimic a denizen of Australasia.

At one point, neither was capable of twisting the other and we had to remain horizontal, running across the floor like a spider, scuttling over the furniture, four legs and four arms contributing to the motion. This was an exceedingly comfortable and efficient mode of travel, but I could never resign myself to an arachnidan mode of existence. I refused to consider it a viable solution to our problem.

Finally we came to an acceptable compromise. "This ridiculous farce earns nothing but bruises. Why not take it in turns to stand upright? I deem that preferable to spinning like a father broken on a bicycle. Do I sound facetious? My similes are all giddy."

"'Tis reasonable. What arrangement do you suggest?"

"On odd days of the month, I will stand and you will droop. On even days, it shall be the other way around."

"Sounds fair. I agree."

"Today is an odd day. Thus it is my turn."

Elusive Plato

He acceded with reasonable grace and I waddled over to his ranks of effulgent bottles. Here, amid the oneirodyniac array, I located unguents and cool myrrhic lotions. I prepared a poultice with Dotty's rag and sat on a gaudy chaise-longue, soothing my brow and occasionally his. While I moaned, the cobra slid from under a cushion and coiled in my lap, gazing down at its incongruously situated master.

I raised the poultice to dash out its scaly intentions, but my calm vagina restrained me. "Twill be a barbarous act. Florence won't bite you now; she knows it would kill me as well. Our cardio-vascular systems are married as obstinately as a woodlouse troubadour and his oniscoid bride. 'Tis the one thing which saves you."

"I do not intend remaining like this forever. For one thing, we can never leave the house. If we are spotted, we will be pressganged into a circus as an ultimate freak. The hemimorphic Hermaphrodite. And God will be intensely annoyed when He finds out."

"'Tis my main worry. Had the melding worked correctly, we'd be free of His influence. His power wouldn't penetrate our magnetic field. As we are, there's no defence from Him; He'll do whatever He can against us. I imagine He'll make the ceiling fall on us, or send a lightning bolt down the chimney in the shape of a swan."

"How long have we got left?"

"Who knows? Heaven is not an especially efficient bureaucracy. 'Tis rife with corruption at all ecstatic levels. There's millions of sinners and only a few hundred avenging angels. The Cherubim-Gestapo just aren't equipped to keep an eye on everyone all the time. But one thing can't be denied: we set ourselves up as peers to Yahweh and failed. No repentance is possible. Lucifer made a similar mistake."

"In that case, we must undo the error before it is noticed. Luckily I have an idea. I need pen and ink."

My vagina sighed. It was plain it did not believe in the likelihood of a workable solution. "We're too far gone. 'Tis self-deception to deny this. The Hermaphrodite is a shambles. Look at our skin!" Fatty globules rolled under the surface of our flesh. "Hard boiled philosophical eggs!" Tears trickled down his brow to the carpet.

I repeated my demands for writing materials; a valid postage stamp was also required. The pudendous savant glumly acceded. Directing me to an especially cluttered corner of the room, I rummaged through spacious cupboards filled with snuff boxes, jars of macédoine, rapiers, casques, walnuts, oboes, toenail clippings, string vests, candelabra, packets of saffron dust, broom handles, unicycle chains, used chamber-pots.

I even found a dismantled blunderbuss, which I reassembled for my amusement. A cardboard box brimming with stationery finally appeared under the junk, odious paper and scented envelopes included.

As I selected materials, I became aware that I was starting to gain some control over the alchemist's limbs, as he was over mine. With great effort, we were able to partly move each other's arms and feet. Thus our flawed fusion, though obviously a blasphemy, was still a genuine melding of nervous systems. It became advisable to view the Hermaphrodite as the archetypal gestalt, needing co-operation to function properly.

At first, we were inclined to play vulgar tricks—I forced my hip-arms to pick my nose. Mark Xeethra Samuels made me scratch my back with Florence. Yet we were mature enough to quickly abandon such pranks.

I sat at a desk and began penning an epistle. My vagina was curious and demanded to know whom I was writing to. I told it to look to its own business—as I was about to do, in one of the chamber-pots removed from the cupboard. When it was the alchemist's turn to relieve himself, I had to hold my tongue to keep it from flapping and shake the yellow droplets from its tip. A thoroughly distasteful process.

Finishing my letter, I signed it with a flourish and sealed it into an envelope. Then I licked a stamp with the remaining traces of urine in my mouth and pressed it firmly down. Crumpling the document into a tight sphere, I inserted it into the blunderbuss.

"What's going on?" My vagina was frustrated. "How can a letter save us? 'Tis a foolish notion! Why are you loading it into an antique gun? I suspect you've lost your fragile reason."

"This epistle is our one hope. You will know who it is addressed to when it is answered. But there is no safe way of posting it; we must not leave the building. Thus the firearm."

There was no gunpowder available in the building, but the macédoine had absorbed nitre from the chamber-pots and was now highly explosive. I used a whole jar to propel my message.

Elusive Plato

Directly opposite the house, on the cracked pavement, a pillar-box stood like a dwarf flagellant. Its mouth gaped invitingly. I raised the window, leaned out and aimed the blunderbuss. The trigger felt less like a woman than a girl. The flint sparked, the charge ignited. There was a roar which deadened my ears; the recoil knocked me backward. The wobbly casement dropped down like a guillotine.

When I righted myself and rushed to the glass, I was gratified to see the sphere entering the maw and disappearing into the pillar-box's gullet. Now it was a question of waiting.

The days passed like swallowed hooks. Even numbers of the calendar were my times of penance. Prime numbers were when I was self-confident beyond endurance. We decided to keep the blunderbuss by our side at all times; there was no telling when God or one of His agents would make a move. We paced the chamber like an aardvark. We used broken glass from the chloroform and dream bottles as ammunition. At infrequent intervals, my vagina begged me to reveal the name and address of my correspondent. But I kept my upper lips tightly sealed.

Domestic chores were made easier by the possession of two pairs of hands. Washing dishes and cleaning the bookshelves were no longer tasks of unimaginable horror; my juggling also improved. Soon we were both so familiar with our misplaced twin that we acquired full control over his bodily parts. I was able to apply his hands and legs as well as my own.

We made another deal: the standing one, for twenty four hours, had sole rights over all limbs. It worked admirably. For defecation and unclean purposes, I relied exclusively on his fingers.

We took up our discourse on philosophy where we had left it. I was allowed to touch, though not open, his shy books; he recited most of his knowledge from memory. A vagina's lectures are enveloping. When his time of the month came, blood seeped from his mouth and he grew surly. I was able to keep him in a good temper by levering his mathematical erudition from his dangling brainpan. He defined the shape known as a tesseract, a curious symbol, both pleasing and unbearable to the eye. This was a form of hypercube, an elevated geometrical figure.

"The tesseract," he said, "is a representation of a gateway between parallel realities. 'Tis a simple cube extruded into the fourth spatial dimension. As such, 'tis not a door in itself but the schematic for one. Who knows the correct medium for its application?"

The shape he directed me to draw, on the Stygian notepaper, was an octagon made up of eight shuffled squares.

"It resembles my family tree," I remarked. "Only a few connections are missing. Here is my grandfather, Leopoldo, and my grandmother, Eva. These lines link with their children: Rosendo, my father, and Carmen, my mother. Here is a crow and a mole."

"You have a history of intermarriage? Your clan reminds me of some rotting Æritreac dynasty. 'Tis horrid!"

I fumed. "For that insult, my ancestors would have strapped you to a housewife and thrown you into the Tagus. Indeed, for carrying out such an operation on the local curate we were banished for many years to the Sierra Morena. It is a dismal region, where innkeepers have been evicted by ghosts, the ghosts by skeletons and the skeletons by innkeepers. When the Conde de Olivarez colonised it, we left."

"'Tis strange to hear of a lineage which bears comparison with such an abstract pattern. Could it be that your family somehow forms part of this gateway between alternative worlds?"

"That sounds flattering. But it makes no sense."

My vagina sighed. It was hungry, so I searched the pantry for more bratwurst. Never before had eating been such pleasure; my vulva devoured the sausage with rhapsodic ripples. When it had finished, it demanded a cigarette. I allowed it to roll some vodka-soaked ginseng; I was growing too tolerant of the alchemist's habits.

"The problem with parallel realities is that, though they might lie right next to us, we can't reach 'em. 'Tis like neighbours divided by a high wall. The most we can do is pound on it with metaphysical fists in the hope they'll catch an echo. Vague messages can be sent this way. The universe next door is trying to tell us about 'friendship', but it can't pass through to us even so much as a sincere smile. The worlds are isolated!"

"So the tesseract, or rather the secret it symbolises, is a catflap from one to the other? Plato was unable to make a hole big enough to let through this particular moggie. He attempted to do so by living in caves and wooing calcium carbonate deposits."

"Of course! He was so square he was a cube! But this didn't go far enough; a tesseract is a hypercube."

Elusive Plato

Suddenly, it was clear to me. The tesseract was a recipe for a type of living which would open up a route between the opposing dimensions. I could not imagine what actions were needed, what form of lifestyle might constitute a hypercubic analogue. Did my family, as my vulva suggested, have anything to do with it? Did the intricate links between generations of Cadizites compose a trigonometric shape? Were the tangents and angles of our relationships mystically empowered? If so, God would surely never forgive the sines of my fathers . . .

Yet a few vital struts of the figure were missing. Until these were added, the gateway would remain unfinished.

My vagina was growing inflamed. "Mayhap an alternative Plato, in an adjacent reality, managed to make contact with our version of the toga'd fellow? The former communicated the idea of 'friendship'; the latter was unable to synthesise the sentiment. It had to be traded. They arranged a fair exchange, but it has not yet been carried out. If we force open the gate, Platonic love will slip into our reality, but we'll lose something in return. 'Tis the purest metaphysic!"

Lighting a cigarette filled with porter-soaked petals, the arms of the alchemist removed a book from a low shelf. Opening it at random, he suspended it from a single page. One side of the unlucky leaf stood for our society; the other side symbolised a parallel world. Both were part of a single text, components of the same scheme, but they were isolated from each other by the page itself.

Both verbose societies housed a blinking silverfish, the cue for a second clever conceit. My labia demonstrated how one insect represented proof of God, while the other represented proof of friendship.

Using the tip of his papelito, the savant burned a hole through the text. With an inaudible cry, the creatures rushed through the rent. Now they occupied reciprocal positions in the volume. I understood this visual metaphor at once; by creating a suitable tesseract and welcoming Platonic love into our universe, we would lose our certain knowledge of God's existence. We might replace it with a less comforting quality: faith. The citizens of Earth would have to learn relativism.

"Twill be a mighty challenge!" my labia spluttered. "But one worthy of our best efforts. Not only will it discharge your personal quest, but also help to keep us safe from God!"

I was pleased he had finally decided to defect to my philosophical agenda. But I was unable to bring myself to inform him that his identity no longer figured in my plans.

He replaced the book—*Emetic Victorians* by Lytton Strychnine—and we resumed our perennial pacing. It was worse for him, not knowing what he was waiting for. My worries were healthily practical: what if my letter did not reach its destination? What if the recipient decided not to answer my summons?

When the savant fell asleep that evening, I returned to the shelves and browsed through the demonstration volume, as well as a dozen others. I was not surprised to find them less shy than he had announced. Indeed, they seemed delighted to be caressed by the gaze of a Spaniard.

The most satisfying of my literary encounters that night were chiefly those books in strictest keeping with the character of phantasm. Without my vagina's consent, I pored over such works as the *Pilgrim's Verruca* of Bunion; the *Limbo and Coconuts* of Gamma-Ray Russell; the *Shipomancy* of Robert Flood; and *The Clapper of the Sun* of Campanologa.

One favourite volume was an octavo edition of *The False Book of Truths*, by the Bishop Wormwood; and there were passages in *Kruptos: the Micropaedia*, about the Muswell Hill satyrs and Oélitists, over which I sat dreaming for minutes. And permit me to mention *Boo Jest,* a fanciful account of Brenda the Skogmann, a living tattoo that decided to go to a flesh-parlour and get an arm, but did not stop there, returning on subsequent occasions to acquire a shoulder for the arm to rest on, and later a torso, head, lower body and legs too, for these things escalate quickly; and now she looks like a real girl who has a tattoo rather than a real tattoo that has a girl.

My biggest delight, however, was found in the perusal of a copy of the manual of a coincidence—the unabridged rituals used in Reverend Delves' church in Horam, bound in crypto-quarto pseudo-Gothic.

During the day, we continued sorting clutter in the cupboard at the end of the chamber. The broom handles were innumerable. Dotty Umlaut had been a compulsive purchaser of cleaning equipment, leaving her old tools behind every time she scoured the savant's house.

Elusive Plato

Talk of the oppressive and oppressed domestic servant led me to wonder aloud what condition her broken body was in. "She is bound to be rotting by now," I remarked. "Do you want the stench to rise from the cellar up the lift shaft? I suggest we descend and dispose of her corpse."

My vagina reluctantly agreed. Setting the dumb waiter's controls to a sensible speed, we called it up and huddled within. It groaned like an indiscretion as it lowered us into the bland reek. A clockwork mechanism of some complexity, as reliable as a blind astrologer, it inspired small confidence in my universal joints. I was grateful to step out into a low room carpeted with thin mists and illuminated by slanting sunlight.

Amid rusting bicycle wheels and dusty plant pots, the smashed body of the cleaner was unavailable. A tunnel the shape of a political prisoner led up and away; through this hole, day poked its pollen-encrusted nose. Dotty Umlaut, in speckless passion, had managed to escape.

"She's always been a hard one to kill," my vagina confessed. "She's scrubbed her way out! And she'll be back!"

"What shall we do?" I had little desire to meet the foul hag again. Indeed, in our present position, it was imperative that no-one saw us. I suggested we block the tunnel up immediately. The alchemist nodded; this was a matter of life and myriad limbs.

To this exhausting end, we shuttled all the statues from chamber to cellar, cramming the wickedest busts of History into Dotty's hole, until her potential means of penetration was impassable. I surmised that Henry Christophe, Vlad Tepes and Francisco Solano López would resist until the last chip of marble. Gilles de Rais alone had no part in the defence. My pudenda explained that his statue was on vacation, a working holiday in the resort of Clacton-on-Sea, where it was helping a Gypsy pier-dweller lure idiot children into a carnivorous tent.

"I do not believe this," I mumbled.

"'Tis is not as unlikely as it seems," replied my labia. "Medieval sages often forged sentient brass heads. Fryer Bacon perfected one which had an amazing ability to hawk candy floss. The deepest mysteries of the occult are as sticky as they are hidden. Consider the transformation of your own speech: from elegant to glutinous! Your charming Spanish lisp, once so provocative, has been circumcised!"

I scowled at this reminder of my tongue. I did not relish having to perform fellatio backward whenever I articulated a syllable. If I spoke too quickly, my meanings spurted and congealed on my chin.

With the aid of his filthy hands, I finished arranging the barricade; we returned to the chamber and disabled the dumb waiter. It did not complain. I rested in a chair; while I enjoyed a light doze, the alchemist enjoyed my feral breasts, roughly fondling them with his fingers.

This was a violation of our agreement. Without hesitation, I reached into my mouth and savagely twisted my tongue, until it spilled a rapid series of hard globules down my neck, each pearl containing a single droplet of blood. After this, my vagina was more wary of my nipples, especially the regrown whiskers. My mammary glands still lap their own milk.

Later, in the middle of a proper sleep, we were awakened by a monumental crash. It was past midnight—his turn to stand—so I could do nothing but let him rush to the window and peer out. The house shook like a query, but the street was deserted. Had God found us at last? Was Dotty trying to force entry with a double-headed mop? Had they formed an alliance against us, a bucket and halo axis?

Cradling our blunderbuss, we unlocked the chamber door and made our way along the corridor and down the steps.

Long wooden splinters littered the floor; the cool night air kissed our fear. Crumbs of rock rolled under our feet. The alchemist scooped up a handful and gingerly sniffed them. "'Tis meteorite dust," he said. "My door has been staved by a falling star."

"God's doing? But He is generally a poor shot."

The savant shook his head, twisting my labia into Hindu corners. "I think it may be natural. A coincidence, of course, but the only sensible explanation. These things do happen; shortly after I left Chaud-Mellé, a meteorite killed a whole banter of engineers."

It seemed his assurances were more for his own benefit than mine. I urged Florence, who had followed us, to return to the chamber. There was no way to repair the door, so we followed her.

Whatever the truth behind this violation of our privacy, the incident unnerved us. We strengthened the chamber door, our last line of defence, with bands of steel cut from saucepans. Soon it was a formidable bulwark against assault, shaming the walls, which seemed pitifully thin in comparison. Our efforts multiplied our worries—now we expected an attack from every side, instead of from the single entrance. We reinforced the walls with torn pots, a desperate substitute for cut pans, which were exhausted. I counted the days on his fingers, saving mine for counting weeks.

Half my hand later, plus three of his digits, I cleared the chamber of thaumaturgical machines and moved the flattest table to the centre of the room. I was standing; the alchemist was dangling. I had finished the books on his shelves, still without his knowledge, rounding off with the naive future-pastoral, *Daftness and Chlorine* by Shortus. He had finished the last sausage and was fretting about prospective famine. We could not go shopping as we were. How would we eat?

"The recipient of my letter," I remarked, "should arrive within the hour. My calculations are infallible."

"Who did you write to? The Guild? What if they don't answer? Twill be back to square zero! 'Tis unsatisfactory."

There was a creak in the passage. Someone had entered the house and climbed the stairs. Though expected, the subsequent knock on the chamber door made me prance in triumph. "What did I tell you? He is here! Now we shall end our abutting relationship!"

"I'm not convinced. Our very quarks are shared!"

The knock was repeated; the knuckles belonged to a man. Ignoring my vagina, I slid open the innumerable bolts. Then I flung wide the portal, preparing to face a friend. Instead, to my horror, I found myself in the proximity of a fiend. The difference is not slight. My bowels slackened; my diarrhoea was literal and verbal—the latter due to the former. As I retreated, the nightmare stated its aims.

"I hávë cômè för my mónthly clëân, Màstër Sâmuéls."

Quick as a Turk, I raised my blunderbuss and pulled the trigger. In the second it took the flint to spark, Dotty Umlaut, monstrously bruised but very much alive, showed her new set of brooms. I retched as I beheld them, a second purging no less dianoetic than my first. Then the Saxonic cleaner advanced and the macédoine ignited.

The broken glass which plugged the barrel discharged into her lumpy face at point blank range. It tore off her whole countenance, her visage disintegrating in the blast.

She tumbled backward into the corridor, her peeled lips framing an incomprehensible question. This time, her accents were driven into her vowels, a semantic acupuncture which helped to cure them of their ailments, so that they enjoyed a longer lifespan than her consonants. This made her scream even more piquant.

I dropped the gun; the alchemist covered his ears with my hands and his eyes with my own. I wailed at this avarice; I also wanted protection from trauma. Shaking, I searched the stairs for her seeping carcass, but it had vanished. Had she cheated death again? We were too low on smashed glass and macédoine to repel a further attack.

My vagina recovered its composure by smoking a score of cigarettes, mostly filled with cider-soaked toenails. I had no composure to recover; it had been swallowed by Florence the previous evening. Yet my feet were soon lacerated by undetected glass. Combined with my earlier purges, top and bottom, this accidental bleeding cleaned my system of toxic humours. Like a Jesuit with a fetish for oases, I started to feel seriously well. I dismissed the incident with a shrug.

"Why did you let her in?" My yoni was not so blasé. "It was obvious she'd return. You're a silly girl."

"Dotty's calluses deceived me. The knock belonged to a man. She has very masculine skin, my friend likewise."

"How can you speak that word in my presence? 'Tis rank presumption! Its inner meaning is quite beyond us."

"I feel able to use it with growing confidence."

Muttering about foolish delusions, my vagina fell into a lubricated sulk. It vowed never to become my friend, even if we were able to open a gateway to let the concept proper through.

While it brooded, a second knock troubled the room. My yoni shouted in panic: "Don't answer! 'Tis Dotty again!

For a moment, I was unsure; then I heard the laugh, the gurgle, and knew we were truly saved. My sex protesting at every step, I reached the door and hauled it open. A bounder stood in the penumbra, tightening his elegant cynicism with a sequence of bows. His voice was a blue mandolin. "Is this the residence of Bartleby Cadiz?"

"Porlock, you butcher! Do you not recognise me?" I embraced him and licked his chin with the alchemist's member. Before I could finish these decent expressions of gratitude, he turned and fled.

Elusive Plato

Launching myself in his wake, I overtook him. The passage was, as I have stated, exactly the height of a man who has legs in place of arms. While my feet ran on the floor, those of the savant ran on the ceiling; thus our speed was twice that of the hapless student surgeon.

Four arms entwined around his waist, I dragged him back to the cell and locked the door. Over and over again, he begged me to let him go. At last, he calmed to the point where he was willing to absorb my words. He squinted in my face and chewed his lip.

"Bartleby, is it really you? I left Brighton as soon as I got your letter. You promised me the most interesting medical case of my career. I never suspected you meant yourself!"

"Did you find London easily enough?"

"I arrived yesterday morning. As you directed, I waited for an odd day before seeking this address out."

"Did you have an eventful journey?"

"Excised a dozen cataracts on the road; hitchhikers are a wondrous source of disease. Served as a nutritious snack on the way." He reached into a pocket and removed a bag of cloudy irises. "Would you like one? I prefer them to epiglottic humbugs."

I declined his offer. "Still a vegetarian, I see. But tell me if my condition is curable. What do you think?"

Small talk disposed, curiosity aroused, Porlock Sniggervalue jabbed my body with his professional fingers. He clucked his tongue, tugged his nose and wiped mucus from both. He was repelled and admiring at the same time. "The first man I've met capable of performing intercourse with his mouth and cunnilingus with his privates!"

My labia was growing uneasy. "Bartleby is a woman! A virgin as pure as a sandal! 'Tis an insult to call her a man. But I'm also a virgin; we constitute the epitome of immaculateness."

At this outburst, Porlock chuckled obscenely and explored friction with his palms. "My fame is assured! What you have here, my darling, is a very rare talking cancer. A chatty sarcoma!"

Disingenuously, I replied: "I have heard that tumours can sometimes resemble limbs. Are you able to remove them?"

"Yes, I think so. With a hacksaw."

Needless to say, the savant was infuriated by the direction of our conversation. He wrung my hip-arms. "Cancer? How dare you? 'Tis a gross mismanagement of perception! I'm none other than Mark

Xeethra Samuels, a brilliant alchemist and smoker. If anyone is a cancer, 'tis this harlot who calls herself an Usher! Perdition!"

I lowered my voice to a resigned whisper. "My disease is delirious. If I am the cancer, why am I standing upright? I beg you to lose no time in amputating its malignant head."

Porlock frowned. "I would like my tutors in college to witness your condition. I don't think I should operate here. Come to Brighton with me and I'll comply with your request."

"But it is growing at a furious rate! What can I offer you to start now? All the treasures in this chamber?"

Porlock snickered. Mucus dripped in artistic spirals on the carpet. "Money isn't much use to me. I've still got your gems, remember? I can't accept such a pitiful bribe. You'll have to do better than that. Science should come before personal comfort."

"I know how to persuade you," I answered. "I have one thing to give you will not refuse." And I mentioned my proposal with a seductive wink. His eyes flashed and he turned the colour of a grilled milkman. A bulge rose in his trousers like a surfacing Zeuglodon. He removed his leather coat and cast it carelessly aside.

Placing his bag of instruments on the floor, he opened it and chose a pertinent blade. Then he bade me prostrate myself on a flat surface. I had arranged the table for this purpose. While I lowered myself, my yoni expressed indignation. "She's a liar! 'Tis a set-up! We can't be divided safely. She plans to kill me! Impiety!"

Porlock strapped me onto the table with his belt and positioned his hacksaw between my legs. "Amazing how credible these oratorical maladies are! I'm almost convinced by its pleas."

"You have forgotten the anaesthetic," I observed.

"Ho! So the patient seeks to instruct the doctor? Anaesthetic won't advance the cause of medicine—it will interfere with my research. Here is an opportunity to record the death screams of a talking cancer during its removal. You must be fully conscious."

I writhed in my bonds. "Rascal!"

It was pointless to struggle. He worked the saw and carved a notch in the alchemist's head, flush with the bottom edge of my pelvis. It was only possible to cut off protruding extremities: my vagina would have to remain a mouth. Blood and shrieks poured from my yoni as Porlock's blade broke through the skull and grazed the dura-mater, the exterior membrane of the brain.

Elusive Plato

The saw slipped at this point and the student had to lever out the tool and wipe the tiny teeth on his sleeve, cleaning away shards of glistening bone. The tone of the saw being wrenched in and out of the savant's cranium was an octave higher than that of a cat being beaten to death with a blackboard. As he sliced deeper, my extra limbs flailed out comically—the gestures of a hebephrenic mummer.

Although in excessive torment, I preserved enough sense to bark an idea at my assailant: "Keep the hip-arms. I might be able to use them."

He nodded and took a brief rest; he had reached the halfway stage. For the first time, I was drenched with an understanding of my own cruelty. Pain is the liberator of all our sins and virtues—but it is facile to discuss it in any low decibel manner.

My vagina's cries had turned into dismal gurglings. The alchemist's mind was a hotel for agony; it booked a double room in both hemispheres and scorned room service. When Porlock returned to his task and finished it, agony went down for breakfast. The head rolled free of my pelvis and fell off the side of the table, its landing cushioned by Florence.

I was able to shut my legs again; in the midst of my troubles, this was a huge relief. My vagina moaned vegetative phrases.

While he was in the region, he made other incisions and extracted a length of intestine, laying it carefully by my side. This was what I had bribed him with—the reward for his trouble. Since our aborted romantic meal, he had lusted for no other cylinder.

After this, the operation went more smoothly. Porlock freshened his blade with viridescent phlegm before tackling the savant's legs. Showers of gore cooled my brow. A sheet of sandpaper was his method of restoring feminine shoulders. Soon they were acceptable to public scrutiny. Only a closer inspection revealed the truth: rings of bone, surrounding circles of marrow like myopic archery targets where the alchemist's femurs in cross section were level with my skin.

As instructed, Porlock left my hip-arms as they were. Exhausted, he reeled away from the makeshift operating-table and sniffed the air. "I'm famished! What's lingering in the larder?"

I was too numbed by my experience to inform him that we were out of food. He started rummaging through the boxes, cupboards and shelves like a selfish Mother Hubbard. As his search continued without success, I saw him grow petulant. "You lulled me here without bothering to purchase any supplies?" He groped behind the dream bottles.

His quest finally led him to the adjacent room, where the alchemist had kept his deficient virgins. He turned the colour of a skinned lawyer as he beheld the pickled women in jars. "Ah, refreshments!" Slapping his belly, he stepped inside. "I'm on a macrobiotic diet. Dairy products are not allowed. I'll leave the breasts for you."

Before he finished his repast, I recuperated sufficiently to squirm out of the belt which lashed me down.

The world still span; it had never really stopped since my Brighton debauch. With the yell of a porpoise, I gained my feet, flexing my stiff muscles. Without the weighty presence of Mark Xeethra Samuels, I felt as light as a landlady. I glanced at Porlock. He sat amid a flood of greasy liquid, having overturned the jars and removed the stoppers. The pickles had all vanished, with the exception of the highwayman, who was dragging himself along the boards by his fingernails.

Porlock eructated fashionably and disregarded his escaping dessert. Picking his teeth with a sinew, he waved at me. "That's better! I'm full up! Now I feel ready to satisfy lower bodily desires." He nodded, a sign for me to bring over my present. I draped the intestine over my arms and presented it to him like a sash of honour. As the owner of two digestive tracts, the loss of one was not too disturbing.

Porlock took it tenderly and pressed it to his lips. Then he stood and dropped his trousers. Like my father and the alchemist, he seemed to eschew underwear. Was I the only inhabitant of the planet who considered privates to need two layers of material to protect them from cruel fate?

I was astounded by the dimensions of the student's scrotum; it resembled an unmilked udder. Doubtless the result of involuntary sexual restraint. I watched in fascination as his member rose from the spherical mass, but he was embarrassed and insisted I leave the room. I respected his wishes and he slammed the door behind me.

When he emerged, three hours later, the change in his lower anatomy was dramatic. His scrotum had shrivelled; his enfeebled member was blue in the face. He dangled my intestine before him, bulging with fluid and secured with an obscure sailor's knot.

Guessing at once it would make an ideal water-bed for Florence, I urged him to lay it down for her. With a grateful hiss, she slithered onto it and fell asleep, like an arrow on a salami. I had grown fond of her scales.

For the third time, there was a noise in the corridor. For once, it was not followed by a knock. The door burst like a scowl and the heathen cleaner stepped over the threshold, loosing a berserker shout. Lacking a face, she resembled a ghost-comedian. I clanked my bloody bones in token apprehension. I was still too sore to feel fear.

"I rëfúsë tô lèävé yôúr sêrvicè, yóü ûngràtëfúl chîmp!"

"Dotty," I answered, "your master is not here. You may take the few leftovers, but I doubt they will make a satisfactory employer. You ought to consider seeking an alternative job. Have you ever thought of working in an office environment? There are some very nice premises in Grovedale Road which are in need of your talents."

"Whát hävê yòü dôné wïth my pôôr álchèmist?"

There was little to be gained from arguing with her. My blunderbuss was useless. I remembered the savant's boast that he had removed a dream from every person he met. I reached the shelves of bottles and picked up the container labelled with her title. Pinned to the wall was a complete list of unfortunates who had lost dreams. A few names, including my own, had been crossed out; I assumed they represented smashed bottles. These deleted cognomens formed a record of the alchemist's outbursts of anger. I noted the appellation of my mortal enemy.

Dotty's bottle was cold to the touch; it had a stem as waggish as a pin. I used my hip-arms to hurl it—they were more vindictive. It broke on her ankles and the oneiric cloud enveloped her so fully that only the tip of her new mop showed above the surface.

The fog contained a scene of horrible warfare. Warriors in barbaric garb ran amok through the streets of a marble city, toppling columns and setting fire to villas. Stained togas and trampled grapes were scattered everywhere. Doubtless this vista was as novel to her as to us; I did not dispute the savant's postulation that dreams were shared between kindred sleepers. Dotty's voice was strained.

"Mëïn Wódën, thê Húns àrê säckïng Rómè wïthôút mè!"

Without lingering for another moment, she turned and raced down the stairs. I gazed out of the window and saw her gathering speed toward the east, wearing an inverted bucket on her head.

As I watched, she leapt to pluck a hovering seagull out of the air, pulling off its wings and tying them to her bucket with a strand weeded from her broom. Then she was off again; a vengeful Valkyrie, high on detergent, low on morals, her stride as ample as that of a Bösendorfer.

One unforeseen consequence of throwing the bottle was the shrapnel which sprinkled the chamber. Turning from the casement, I kicked pieces of sharp glass across the floor. While Porlock chuckled, one glittering edge punctured the pressurised intestine; it exploded with the elegance of an enema. Florence was propelled at high velocity across the room on the crest of a seminal wave. She speared into the student's thigh.

With a venomous oath, he fell and clutched at his leg. I ran to his side and tugged at the cobra. Florence was buried deep; she asphyxiated before I managed to extract her. Porlock's wound was Chinese in flavour—yellow at the edges and only to be probed gingerly.

I helped him to a sitting posture and tended him with the thumbs of a nurse. He was unable to stand without aid, but my practicality came to garrotte his difficulties. Starched, Florence made an excellent walking stick.

The wound did not heal cleanly; it festered and a fever set in. I wrapped him in his leather coat and listened to his ceaseless rant as he deliriously circled the chamber. When the heat subsided, he neglected to renew his subscription to sanity. The screws of his intellect now missed a thread; he was not the man I knew and loathed. He was a different kind of Porlock, equally hateful but less shy.

Dotty's borrowed dream inspired in me a nostalgia for Roman attire. I stitched a selection of the scrubber's rags into a loincloth and spent much time parading before a wardrobe mirror.

With a string vest as a net and a trident made from a gold candelabrum tied to a broom handle, I was the very figure of a gladiator, a proud Retiarius. My trident had an odd outlook for a thrusting weapon; the standard models are generous, giving wounds and expecting nothing in return. But my spikes were hollow spaces where tallows were supposed to reside. Puncturing flesh, they would take samples from the sub-strata of an adversary.

While I flirted with the silvered glass, Porlock crouched jealously on a rival wardrobe. He distrusted stony artifice. My unique shape, with its quaestorial limits, resembled a Proterozoic growth that had refused to fossilise. When the freshman doctor made stale gestures with capsized thumbs, the effect was as poor as the debt-agony of a bankrupt province. I growled with the gums of a patrician.

"Preserve some respect. You are insulting the man who almost became the left side of a divine Hermaphrodite."

I realised my mistake immediately, but he hissed like a tree doomed to burn a witch. "Now I understand! It wasn't a carcinoma after all! You tricked me with feminine wiles. I'll tell God about your treachery. I'll receive an ample reward for my pains: perhaps He'll make me Prophylactic Minister in Heaven. You monstrous vermin!"

Devoid of meaningful testicles, leather coat shining, walking stick tapping a rousing rhythm on the boards, he limped toward me and breached my pure aura with a twisted expression. I sought out his weak thigh with my trident; he jumped back and retracted his frown.

Now I had him on the run. Florence, though an ophidian épée, was no match for my triple lunge and quadruple armipotence. I approached the surgeon, preparing to strike him off the register of living beings.

He was saved by the postman. The fellow knocked loudly, but entered without awaiting a reply—an outrage graded between the cleaner's first and second resurrected visits. Incredibly, it was the same messenger who delivered the alchemist's letter to my mother. My tip had enabled him to buy a superior round in London. While he handed me a parcel, Porlock saw the chance to slip away. He took it.

My curiosity overcame my bloodlust; I tore open the package as soon as the courier departed. The wrapping had been sealed with Gypsy sweat. Inside, a granite head winked and spat a cheque from its mouth: payment from a pier-dweller in Clacton-on-Sea. Tanned and invigorated, the bust of Gilles de Rais was back from holiday. By the time I found a place to pocket the sum, Porlock was irrecoverable.

I fretted. I knew he was serious about informing God of the aborted coup. Highgate was no longer an appropriate residence; I had to leave as soon as possible. But where would I find refuge? I stuffed my loincloth with the most practical items in the house: a chamber-pot, the packet of saffron dust, the sentient statue.

Then I briefed my feet on the arduous mission ahead. A long amble was in store. There is only one place in the whole world safe from Gods and Councils. It is a sanctuary infested with salacious moles, where eaves drip like keys.

The journey back to Horam was a rite of passage in reverse. I felt like a Sioux sun dancer having his nipples returned. My yoni was a poor travelling companion, uttering turgid groans at each call of nature.

My extra arms folded under my loincloth, net and trident drinking the dew, cat brassière flashing in the sun, I was a Spartacist oiled with Latian wisdom. Gilles de Rais spoke little English and less Spanish; we talked in odours. His pheromones made Esperanto look partisan.

I took a direct route home, leaping hedges and horses. Scratched on briars, sprained in ditches, my ankles attracted the thirsty attention of yokels, who liked to compare their beauty with cider.

Where my path coincided with a road, I attempted to hitch a lift. A gruelling task for my thumb—the drivers of carts were suspicious of my beard, which had grown into a miser's fork.

On the turnpikes of Surrey, I met sundry travellers, mainly buskers and herbalists. I stole food and songs from them after dark; they trusted me as if I was a melody. Towns east of Dorking, site of the defused Armageddon, welcomed my curves; yet I still held on to my virginity, refusing to talk to bakers and tailors. My hips were as frosty as Æstoniac knives.

Crossing the border into Sussex involved picking through the barbed wire fences and crawling past the sentries on my belly. My brief sojourn with Florence had taught me all I needed to know about slithering.

Poked full of holes by the cruel twists of metal, I became a source of protein for bats, who clung to my body and shrouded my alluring form in leathery apparel. In turn, Gilles de Rais feasted on these creatures; I felt like a harlequin whose motley is composed of livers instead of lozenges. But a regular change of clothes is healthy. Only when we broached the Nature Reserve north of Charlwood, where the bats were joined by flamingos, did I grumble. Pink is the heaviest colour.

Elusive Plato

When I was quite sure I was alone, I undid my loincloth and allowed my extra arms to stretch themselves. Once I was spotted by the player of a ukelele, a pariah among the troubadour world. I broke his neck and his instrument at the same time. I sold the strings to a hangman, who wanted them for dangling pianists.

I was never lonely on this voyage; brothers and sisters of the road lurked in copses, calling beautiful greetings. I showered petals over them and played dice with lentils. The girls danced only on their toes, lovely as the choreography of a fit. Because my life is one where unlikelihoods pace the cloisters of my identity, I remained unperturbed by the sequence of coincidental encounters, three in number, that followed, in miniature Markly Wood.

The first concerned a stunted fellow, groping his way through trees no taller than he. I recognised his eyeless visor at once; I was pleased as a gouge to see him. He heard my footfall but was at a disadvantage; I netted him with a single cast of my string vest.

As he flapped ungainly, I spoke his name. He pounded his blue fists on the ground and shouted an abridged oath. "Cobalt Hugh!" I repeated. "As a result of your advice, I joined the Ushers and was kidnapped by a mad alchemist. Now God is after me and I hold you ultimately responsible."

He was exasperated. "How can you blame me for that?"

I shrugged. "It is not difficult. The Cadiz family have made an art of grudges. Remove your mask, varlet!"

"I can't. After we parted company, I did a roaring business at the *venatione*. I made so much money I was able to stuff my face with cakes. My cheeks expanded and this demonstration visor became stuck. I'm going back to Dover, but can't find my way."

I laughed. His stomach had also grown in size; I prodded it with my trident. "You have wandered into the wrong county!" Instead of receiving this knowledge with orthodox despair, he lunged blindly at me and caught my loincloth with his chubby fingers. As he tugged it, my hidden effects cascaded out: the chamber-pot shattered, setting up a resonant frequency in his mask, which also broke; the packet of saffron dust burst like the shell of a pagoda. A cloud of yellow spice blew up in a whimsical breeze and dusted him like a parsnip in satori.

At the same time, I thrust again with my weapon. The candelabrum is an underrated means of offence. It bit deep into the subcutaneous fat of his eminent gut. When I withdrew the prongs, the ensuing vacuum wrenched out three pillars of glistening tallow, threaded with arteries.

With the reduced shriek of a stool among chairs, he thumbed the trilogy of shafts in his abdomen. Realisation jumped over his countenance; small hops. The belladonna I had earlier tried to poison him with seeped to the surface. He saw this and felt doubly betrayed.

"I used to be a blue dwarf. But you've turned me into a yellow imp! Now I'll have to go and live in Monmouth!"

Without further ado, he rushed off and I generously made no attempt to haul him back and complete my task. I inspected my trident. Later, in the evening, I rubbed twigs together and lit the embedded arteries. As I anticipated, they made excellent wicks for the artisan's candles.

Thus I was able to illuminate my way into the centre of the forest, moonless as it was, leaving in my wake the rumour of a landlocked Neptune visiting a Sylvan cousin. When the sun rose, my tallows sputtered and died: I found myself on the banks of the River Rother.

The blonde Personnel Officer was washing her hair in the waters. As second unlikely meetings are usually more profitable than first ones, my manners were perfect. I bowed and addressed her with formal charm. There was a moment in which her reflection recognised me but her real self did not; then she jumped up, split ends dripping over her anger.

With verbal abuse so savage the very words were cowed, she denounced my existence. I waited for her to pause and then clutched her to my bosom. She melted in my embrace and nibbled the ends of my soft beard.

"Oh, Bartleby! Why did you defect? You are the first Usher to leave the Guild during a hunt. You can't conceive the disgrace it brought down on my head! I was forced to resign."

"But what are you doing in Sussex?"

"I'm on my way to Brighton. There's a famous seminary in that town. It needs carpenters to replace a missing desk. I'm applying for the job. Like all virgins, I'm handy with a bradawl."

"You tried to proposition me the night before the *venatione*. I wish to know if the offer still stands."

"I suppose so. Your beard is certainly gorgeous. But I mustn't lose my woodworking skills for the sake of an orgasm. Is frottage acceptable, do you think? Or does it count as coitus?"

I sighed. I did not know the answer to this riddle. Having gained a measure of respect for fellow humans in the previous weeks, I was loathe to ruin her prospects. I decided to forgo my pleasure. I had waited many months for a sapphic release; I knew I could wait a little longer.

These moral stirrings within my latticed bosom should have made my name ignite with shame, but I was ready to change the world and even the howls of my ancestors in my blood could not encourage me to violate her. We lay down in the mossy undergrowth and fell asleep in each other's arms

My beard, half of which was the alchemist's pubic hair, made a blanket for breasts and moods. My sleep was faster than hers; my dreams raced across my lids with the urgency of chewed clouds.

While I slumbered, my extra arms were busy, inserting knuckles into the corners of her eyes. Without my permission, they were extracting her visions, remembering a former purpose. When my own fantasies dissipated, having rained themselves out, I rose to find the burst packet of saffron dust full of the colleagues of her dream.

I folded my hip-limbs, binding them more tightly into the loincloth, and kissed the Personnel Officer's ear. She stirred sluggishly and smiled, but did not wake. A golden misty morning seeped through the expurgated forest. Needing to relieve myself, I took my tongue to the banks of the river. Unbuttoning my face, I poked my organ and stooped to empty my chest-bladder.

The barge loomed out of the coiling vapours like a tramp's curse in a miasma of gin. I waved to it, using my brassière as a heliograph—the favourite form of communication for a hellion. I saw a chance to travel the last stretch to Horam in style. The bargee— whose form I could not see—directed his vessel toward me. I took this as an offer of warm welcome.

With a moderate leap, I launched myself from bank to deck. Only a little stagger awaited me on the polished boards; I made my way toward the wheelhouse to pay homage to my host.

The grinning visage of a familiar smuggler thrust out and gave vent to a savage hooting. I tried to retrace my steps, my jump, but the barge had already pulled back to the centre of the stream. Beyond the reeds, I saw a flash of blonde and wept. I had discarded my second—and possibly final—chance to have a fulfilling lesbian experience.

While I stood on the rim of the vessel, a single arm seized me from behind and dragged me back to the bridge. The rudder, I saw, was lashed with celery woven into rope. Again I was tied to a hammock by my nipple whiskers, while a warty accent scraped away my pleas for clemency.

"Quarter, is it? You Whore of Brighton! You stole my hand!" Captain Nothing tore my loincloth and gasped at the sight of my hip-arms. "I see now! You collect 'em! Which one's mine, eh?" And he tugged at both right and left auxiliary wrists, as if determined to uproot them. "I've waited ages for this! Come on, you deceitful tart!"

"Neither of those hands belongs to you," I explained patiently. "I left yours in the deeps of my vagina."

"Oh yes? You'll be sorry you tricked me before. I may be a Nullity, but I'm no empty-headed walrus. Open your legs and let's see! If I can't find it, I'll take your four in exchange."

It was useless to resist. Wedging open my thighs with a sextant, he applied an eye to the aperture. "Can't see a blasted thing. It's as dark as slavery in there! Hullo?" He called into my yoni and listened for the echo. "Yes, there's something inside!"

Before I could tell him that it was my tongue, he opened a chest in the corner of the room and withdrew a curious clockwork device. He wound it up and moved it over my buttocks and labia.

"A metal detector!" he cried. "I'm not going to be caught out by an intrauterine gin-trap again!" Leaning forward, he added: "You managed to burn my ship, destroy my career, singe my flesh, but I never resigned. I sold the salvage rights and bought this miserable hulk. Now I run garden vegetables between hydrophobic misers. But I'll work my way back up; the first step is retrieving my prodigal fist!"

It did not occur to him that, were it still stuck in my cervix, his hand would have fermented by now. My fallopian tubes would be awash with palm wine, a heady brew for the muff diver. He finished with the strange instrument and nodded. "The metal detector says you're clear. No need to worry about gynaecological molars. Oh, Bartleby! Why did it have to come to this? I molested in good faith!"

Quick as a brute, he thrust his good arm into my depths. Some acts are so remarkable that Nature seems determined to repeat them. The real teeth of the savant now closed on his wrist. Severing this hand was not as easy; my incisors were blunt.

With extravagant gyrations of my hips, exotic as those of a Cairene crab, I succeeded in separating the rapist from the rape. His shout contained so much disappointment that his mass was not lessened by the amputation. Indeed, it multiplied. I cauterised the wound with smarting wit. "Hands off!"

He fell back, stumps waving in the air. I wrenched myself from the hammock, leaving a second set of cat's whiskers tangled in the weave. I did not think, despite this growing collection, he would ever fine tune a future reception for me.

He rushed out of the cabin and I followed. A freak wind had blown us once more close to the bank. To my amazement, I saw the blonde Personnel Officer wading through the current. She gained the side of the barge and climbed aboard.

"Bartleby! What's going on? I looked everywhere for you. I seem to have lost a dream. I'm not refreshed."

Before I could answer, the crippled Captain Nothing yelled: "I bet it was stolen by this bitch. She took my arms!" And he attempted a kick at my yoni. But my hip-arms caught his foot and propelled him backward. He hopped like a jester with an untuned hat.

"It is true," I admitted, with a manifold shrug.

"You recidivist!" The Personnel Officer rushed to Captain Nothing's side and stabilised him. For a moment, her arms were threaded under his shoulders, giving him the appearance of a Hindu avatar with leprosy. She continued to heap abuse on my lovely head. It was time to retire. "Tart! Gross trollop! Harlot! Iberian strudel!"

The smuggler was ecstatic in her embrace. She clutched him tighter and started tasting his nape, which unlike mine was not perforated with an alchemist's anus. Then he whirled and fell upon her, while she moaned with delight and ate his beard, a coarser bush than mine.

Ignored by my former lover and assailant, I sadly departed, leaping comfortably to dry land, while the barge sailed on, powered by a mounting orgasm. Only once did I look back; the Captain had penetrated the virgin and blood covered the deck. Then the couple withdrew from my life.

Thus ended my third unlikely encounter. My depression lifted with a realisation I was close to my goal. But I needed to expunge my affection for the Personnel Officer; I emptied the packet of saffron dust into the muddy waters. Her dream reacted with the liquid, bubbling on the surface like a divorcee. In that revealing meniscus, I saw Marlow Nothing on his knees, praying to God.

By some remarkable coincidence, the Chief Usher's dream had brought home one belonging to the smuggler. As both palms were still in his possession, I knew this was a dream from a time prior to my first meeting with him. He was asking the Deity for a girlfriend. He had described this scene to me on the tramp, insisting I was the chosen one. Now I knew God had reserved the Personnel Officer for his delectation. I shook at this reminder of the Deity's propinquity.

The savour of fear on the tip of my vagina, I continued my journey. Markly Wood lies just to the north of Horam. One more day passed; I entered the village on Sunday morning.

The houses winked at me like dead fish. I felt like a frog wearing the skin of a tadpole—the comforts of an amphibian womb, the most blessed oxymoron, awaited. Not forgetting my manners, I curtsied in greeting; the cider breweries exuded seven odours of cyanide—only pips are brewed in Sussex. The curio shops and brothel were as I left them, nine months previously.

Exactly three-quarters of a year had passed since I boarded a train for Brighton. Such a short time! Yet much had happened in that period—not least my challenging of God's divine rule. What would Mother say?

Gaining the grounds of my house, I strolled across the garden. As I was about to step over my sister's grave, the moist soil stirred; a tiny arm emerged. Something was clawing its way out of the Bösendorfer coffin with unseemly haste. I knew what it was, of course, and bent to pluck it from the earth.

I had no teeth in my mouth to cut the umbilical cord; my yoni was busy sucking a thumb. So I pulled it out of the grave like some gargantuan tape-worm. As if connected to the subterranean piano—rather than to its occupant—the line sounded a poignant note. Linked with the wail of the creature in my arms, and my own cry of joy, I do not need to explain that the resultant chord was an umbilical joining me to father's insanity. My hip-arms slapped my own buttocks.

Cradled in the crook of my elbow, the filthy being settled into the mature lamentations of a philosopher. It was showing precocious ability. I shifted my trident to a lower hand and knocked on the door of my home. It is best not to elucidate my emotions at this point. I waited with two pairs of trembling lips and percussive knees.

The portal swung like a dislocated jaw. My mother, completely naked save for a tattooed fig leaf, regarded me with two more strands of white in her jackdaw hair; she had aged a notch. She was the image of the very first housewife, who dusted Eden.

The harrowing stench of tinned peaches buffeted my nose. It was the Sabbath: thin cream could be heard gargling in the background. She parted my beard with her fingers and planted nine kisses on my lips. "Bartleby! My son!"

"Daughter," I corrected. I accepted her embrace and rubbed her fake fig-leaf. "Why are you dressed like Adam's spouse? Is this not heresy? I am already in enough trouble with God."

She shook her noble head and noticed the creature on my arm. "Where did you get that? It's riddled with worms!"

"This is your grandson," I announced. "It was born from my sister's grave. Nine months ago, to the day, we buried her. When I prised her off father's stool, I used my favourite knife as a lever; I thrust the blade into her vagina. But it was coated with father's seed. Remember when you gave me his sperm to pour over my peaches? I regurgitated it into a silk napkin and kept it safe. I wiped the knife with the napkin. You are both grandmother and aunt to this child."

"Oh, Bartleby! You were always a rascal!"

She invited me in and we passed through the hallway. I noticed that the astrological clock was back in place, chiming ominously. "But I used it to pay the housewife from the brothel!"

"It's not the same one. I've also been up to reproductive tricks. I seduced the stolen alarm clock. It went off inside me; I became pregnant with time. Yesterday I gave birth to this marvellous example of delicate craftsmanship. Just look at the pendulum!"

"Bulbous as a miser. I saw you and the alarm clock in bed together. I sneaked into your bedroom that night."

"Shame! You're a pervert and violator!"

We laughed; it was almost like old times. The subtle differences in atmosphere raised the hairs on my hip-arms—though not on my own. There was certainly something wrong, but it was so vague a feeling I could not put one of my sixteen fingers on it.

The house looked the same: where my father hung himself, the bannister was still in mourning. But characters were flexing; my mother had altered in some indescribable way. I thought about what Mark Xeethra Samuels had suggested: that my family tree might be a physical analogue of a tesseract, the gate between parallel worlds. If so, two more struts of the shape had been completed—my sister's son and my mother's horological progeny.

"There's someone else I want you to meet," she said. "It might come as something of a shock. Gird your loins . . . "

"Which ones?" I was genuinely confused.

Entering the dining room, I rolled my eyes in disbelief. Perched on an oak chair at the table, spoon raised over a bowl of abominable fruit, as if in benediction, the arch-enemy of our family glanced up and loosed his stained dog collar. His jar stood by his side, uncovered. He clubbed a peach with his eating implement and listened to it thrash in the cream like a seal. Then he smiled and nodded.

"Young Bartleby? Now I recognise you! How did you turn into a girl? You were very cunning at the *venatione!*"

I frowned at mother. "What is he doing here? He loathes our dynasty with excessive zeal. He denounced father's piano as an instrument of the Devil. Every true believer knows that Satan plays the violin. You are as mad as the ancestor whose name I bear!"

The Reverend Douglas Delves stood up. Like my mother, he was naked. A tattooed fig leaf covered his privates also. He beckoned to my mother, who rushed to his side and allowed herself to enjoy his Anglican thumbs. "The Delves and Cadiz families are reconciled," he proclaimed.

Exploring mother's depths more roughly, he encouraged her to moisten. The episode, with its dripping Eve, the lust-obsessed Adam who groped her, resembled an Archean growth that had refused to fossilise—a sickening crystal. When mother received the Reverend's lingam in her mouth, the effect was as blistered as the torso of a melting alchemist.

I allowed them to finish; the seed of Delves was black. I lifted my trident and demanded: "When did we become allies? How did it happen? God is already furious with us. This is the limit."

Delves withdrew from mother and waited for his manroot to deflate. When the blood returned to his body, he folded it between his thighs and adjusted his dog collar, his one item of conventional clothing.

Patting his jar, he replied: "Yahweh no longer exists. But before

I go into more detail about this, I'll answer your other question. Our families decided to sue for peace because of my flask. When I assaulted you in Highgate, you claimed my pickling jar was having an affair. Rushing back, I found your words were true. It was sexually involved with one of your bottles. Naturally, I disapproved of the liaison as strongly as did your mother. But they were obviously deep in love . . . "

"It was the tiny bottle which held your father's issue," my mother added, "after he hung himself. There was still a trace of semen left on the rim. The Reverend's pickling jar was made pregnant. This was how we came together. We lost the heart for fighting. It was but his name that was my enemy. What's Delves? It's not hand, nor foot, nor arm, nor face, nor any other part belonging to a priest. That which we call heretic by any other name would burn as bright."

I lowered my weapon and pouted. "But I had no idea about the glassy tryst. It was a guess, a stab in the dusk."

The Reverend Delves shrugged. "It conformed to a dream I had, so I took your word for it. Come and have a closer look at my jar. There is a smaller jar inside it. An embryo!"

I understood now that my desperate ploy in the *venatione* had worked more effectively than I imagined. By his own account, the savant had met Reverend Delves before, in Chaud-Mellé. He had snatched a dream from the Anglican to add to his collection. But the bottle he kept it in had been smashed—I recalled the deleted names on his list. The dream had wafted out of the chamber and rejoined Delves, who was also in Highgate. But it was not one of his own: the alchemist had proved that our fantasies work for a living and invite colleagues back to the sleeper's head. The dream had belonged to the pickling jar itself.

The coincidence was so staggering, I accepted the offer of studying the pregnancy. Delves had not lied—there was an inner jar, transmuting into the shape of a Klein bottle. And inside this jar, I dimly perceived the elements of a printing press in their fundamental, unformed state. I guessed that this flask, when born, would be capable of breeding magical textbooks and grimoires. Placing my eye to the glass belly, distorted by pressure, I observed the miracle of life.

"But the foetus has no bung!" I pointed out. "What sort of jar will it grow into without a loving stopper?"

My mother was on hand to allay my fears. She reached into her mouth and took a familiar object from her cheek. It was the housewife's nipple which had surfaced in the flooded cellar. Stretching it like a song, she said: "When you left, I decided not to use it as a metronome; it doesn't keep steady time. It's more suitable as a plug for the small jar. My icy saliva preserves it from putrefaction."

I collapsed onto a chair and mopped my brow with the soiled baby. I set it on the table and dipped into my loincloth. I eased Gilles de Rais out of his confinement and handed him to my mother. "A present for you," I lied. "A little something from my travels."

She was delighted. "Best keep him apart from the child! He was good to our family in the fifteenth century."

I inclined my head. "Explain this idiocy about the non-existence of God. The gateway between the dimensions has not yet been forced. Perhaps our universe is already changing as the tesseract nears completion? What do you know of Heaven's recent condition?"

Reverend Delves tapped his nose. "Your words are obscure. Yahweh is no longer in charge of heaven; He has been expelled. The angels war with each other for succession. Cloud Marshal Gabriel has fled to Limbo. Even Saint Peter has abandoned his post."

He described the chaos in Paradise with extravagant gestures. I was able to picture the disorder as if it was taking place on our lawns. The Palace of God had been torn down; the Pearly Gates had been stripped and welded into modern sculpture; the wallets of the holy had been subjected to all manner of indignities. Angels ran amok, looting and fighting with unsheathed harps. I was appalled.

"So Heaven resembles Yorkshire? How did it happen?"

Delves leaned forward, stroking his chin. "That's the peculiar bit. As you know, God used to take holidays in the minds of his followers. It seems that some months ago, he descended from Heaven into the brain of a favourite devotee. But the fellow unwittingly got himself drunk and span Yahweh out of the Universe. He left a smear like butter right across the firmament. We haven't been able to trace the person responsible yet, but we've narrowed his home down to Brighton."

I swallowed with difficulty. "I see."

"God left a diary of engagements. Some things have been carried out by His son—the granting of girlfriends, for example—but the quantity of work is crucifying Him. He's thinking about making a pact with Satan. Until then, Reality belongs to us!"

I decided to change the topic, but only on a lateral plane. Even as I explained the delights of four-dimensional geometry, my own excitement about its applications grew: I had no doubts that the Cadiz family was a route between the dimensions. The portal was already ajar. When a friend enters a room, he does not come through all at once—first he pokes his foot, then the leg appears, then the torso and finally the greeting, the idea of the visit. If you are really lucky, the friend is a girl and her breasts precede her banter.

The tesseract was so close to completion, it was bulging. The certainty of God's existence had departed, like a foot; soon Platonic love would stamp into our world.

Reverend Delves was quick to grasp the concept. "This explains some odd changes. For instance, your mother and I experienced a powerful urge to cast off our normal clothing. But there wasn't a subsequent desire to replace it with anything. So we prance naked!"

"Perhaps," I ventured, "when the gateway is ready, the rest of your compulsion will follow. I believe it will be the need to wear a toga. In a Platonic world, our fashions will billow!"

"I've noticed other discrepancies," my mother interposed. "It seems that even language is altering. Similes are starting to consist of valid comparisons, rather than relying just on musical effect." She raised her fingers and wiggled them. "How do they flap?"

"Like pies!" I cried. Somehow, it was an inadequate analogy. Trying again, I suggested: "Like lips? Like vampires?"

She nodded. "Almost. You're nearly there. The thumbs of an Anglican no longer have the manners of a Quaker's toes."

We exchanged bemused glances. If grammar was doomed to have meaning as well as harmony, what place for mystics, hippies, salesmen, liberals, poets, publishers, dentists, sisters, therapists, lawyers, electricians, waiters, plumbers, dancers, neighbours? Their present status would erode to nothing. I was too hungry to consider this matter further.

I asked my mother for victuals. Tinned peaches were all that was available. Stunned by the horror, but willing to elevate my stomach's needs over those of a jaded palate, I accepted a bowl, slaying the globes with my fists. Still despicable to tongues, they were smooth on a lingam. Surprisingly, I was able to hold them down without retching.

While I swallowed the pyretic repast, I was startled by a grumbling sound unconnected with my belly. It emanated from directly beneath me. I looked down, but saw only the flagstones of the dining room, worn with a dozen generations of Cadizite feasting.

The source of the noise could be located in the flooded cellar which lapped under my feet. Cellars rarely express hunger in such an anthropomorphic way: something was rising from the digestive depths. My sister's son—my nephew—turned its head with a sly look. As like attracts like, this granted me a clue; I wiped mouth and patience on my loincloth and hefted my trident. "Sounds like a child is ascending below. What can this mean?"

Mother was less dumbfounded than the occasion warranted. As I stood and walked toward the basement steps, she accompanied me. Delves fell in behind her. The three of us opened the rusty door and crept down into an eerie gloom.

Before our very squints, an infant broke the waters, a baby with fins. Our house was a focus of fecundity! Reaching the slimy shore, I cast my string vest and tried to net it, but it was out of range. "One of you will have to dive in," I said. "Any volunteers?" I explained that since becoming a flawed Hermaphrodite, with an extra throat in my secret regions, water was liable to choke my yoni.

"I am no longer buoyant," my mother replied. "Reverend Delves and I were married a week ago in a decadent ceremony. Foxes and moles attended the reception. We drank the sourest vintage."

"A housewife?" I was aghast. I did not bother to ask Delves for his excuse. It was obvious, from the way he was whimpering, that I could not expect him to dip a toe. "What shall we do?"

The diving suit which had decorated father's wall was still in fine working order. There was nothing for it but to enlist the help of Gilles de Rais. I inflated the suit with my fetid breath, fixed the bust to the rubber neck and sent him on his way.

The finned infant swam in desperate circles, but was no match for the evil statue's determination to catch a child. The historical monster brought his prize to our feet and licked a stony set of teeth. I wagged a chiding finger and punctured him with the trident. His lust deflated with his ersatz body; we locked him in a cage once belonging to a Khazar parrot.

I placed this new child next to the old. "What was it doing down in the cellar? Did you try to feed it to your abortion, the nameless horror which lives in the chest? Has it escaped?"

My mother shook her head. "I guessed this might happen. You enticed a harlot from a brothel into the cellar and sacrificed her to the beast. But it did not devour her; they copulated and this is the result. As you said, exactly nine months have passed . . . "

"The abortion was a sperm-like abomination!"

"That's right. And the prostitute was an egg. Remember I told you I laid a housewife, but not in water? That was your harlot. Housewives are eggs. When they are fresh, when they honour and obey, they sink. As time goes by, they rot into divorcees, who float."

I grew excited by this revelation. Diving into the cellar to snatch my inheritance, I had witnessed the abortion copulating with the whore, but I never expected it to fertilise her. Yet another part of the mystic tesseract had been formed; there were now only two missing limbs. These presented problems: to create the next angle of the shape, both infants had to couple and produce a baby of their own. Then to finally close the cube, it was necessary for their child to eventually enjoy congress with myself. Only when I sired workable issue, would the quiddity of Platonic Love impinge on our reality.

I babbled out my concerns to my pupils, which is what my mother and the Reverend Delves had become: "Both these children are boys. They will never be able to impregnate each other."

There seemed no way around this paradox. I mulled the conundrum for days. These days turned into weeks, and I found the intellectual fencing involved in the problem unexpectedly restful on my bones. Mental anxiety is a skilled masseuse—but only for Hermaphrodites.

I took to my haunts on the roof, leaping from chimney to trees. My hip-arms made climbing so easy it lost much of its savour. Occasionally, I walked into Horam, to obtain groceries and news. As God no longer existed, I was as free to stalk abroad as horror and fatality. Rumours of God's expulsion filtered into the general consciousness over a period of several months.

Deprived of Absolutism, the burghers and buggers of Sussex started rioting. For a society to function properly, either God or Friendship must exist. I had succeeded in dismissing the former, in the hope of receiving the latter, but had only half-completed the task.

If Plato did not materialise soon, the forces of Nihilism would triumph.

Others were desperately seeking to restore order. I heard a tale of a seaboard college which had set up a provisional Heaven. By the garbled accounts I received in the village pub, it was an oasis of vegetarianism ruled by a muciferous surgeon with a limp.

This seemed a backward step. I had to persist with picking the lock of the dimensional gateway. On the dining room table, once the obnoxious peaches were banished, the Reverend and I pored over metamagical charts, parading tesseracts of various sizes and flavours; with a copper chisel, we inscribed one on the brow of Gilles de Rais. It helped us to focus on the sharper meaning of each angle.

My mother was less helpful. She rated algebra over kisses, but held geometry in utter contempt. "A lower class of trigonometry," she cried. I helped modify her arrogance with a funnel and sundry bottles of obtuse sherry.

I explained my project in lateral terms. She listened with interest as I pointed out the extreme corruption of the Cadiz family. "We refined our turpitude over centuries. Mark Xeethra Samuels, on the other lingam, was a professional virgin. Even his shadow never touched a thigh. Wedded to my own chastity, he attained the zenith of purity. This Hermaphrodite is the epitome of Spiritual Love, whereas Cadizite genes converge toward an ultimate Carnality. From a final mixing of the two extremes, a middle way will be born— Platonic Love."

I had satisfied her like a truncheon, but my speech did not inspire confidence in my ability to make offspring from two males. Yet I was to be helped.

Returning from the tavern one evening, after consuming vast amounts of Amontillado in my tawny confusion, I chanced upon the infants—Wormy and Subaqua, as we had christened them— cavorting over father's tomb. I hid in the shadows and watched them.

They had both matured in an inhuman fashion, reaching puberty before learning to speak. They were digging up his body, taking it in turns to scrabble at the tuneless soil. "Ghouls!" I fumed. But I realised they were making a bed in which to plant flowers of evil: perverted and mouldy strokes.

When they reached the level of my decayed pater, the finned one stretched his crooked form along the bones and allowed my vermiculated nephew access to his nether regions. I could hardly conceive a more disgusting vista.

With a shudder, Wormy discharged into his cousin. The vigour of his climax seemed to drain him completely, leaving him a deflated shell. His lover stood and noticed me. Bloated, he giggled horribly. I snatched him in my arms and rushed into the house to inform Delves of the sight. Much to my relief, the Reverend had an answer:

"The tesseract is helping to create itself. We've reached the point where it can't be halted. Under its own weight, it's swinging open! Laws of Nature are warping to accommodate it. The struts of the hypercube are completed. Only one angle is left to join: Bartleby Cadiz must mate with Wormy's child. Your foetus will be Plato!"

"Physical axioms have certainly become more sprightly," I conceded. "The pace of events has increased massively. When a friend opens a door, he begins slowly, unsure of what is behind. Then he pushes harder: until the door is travelling as fast as an owl. But the final angle is made of three struts. What does that mean?"

"Supreme Purity and Conclusive Corruption are nothing without Time. You must make love inside a clock."

Needless to say, as Plato was so eager to cross into our dimension, Subaqua's pregnancy was of extremely short duration. The foetus expanded in his lower bowel; his buttocks swelled in rhythm. He gave birth during a Sunday meal, collapsing on the table and ripping off his trousers in a threnody of agony. While we watched, his buttocks exploded, showering us with glutinous fat and beige ichor.

The baby was propelled out of his alimentary canal in a devastating arc, missing the ceiling by inches. I raced across the room, string vest in hand and managed to net it. It was a girl, like myself. To polish the allusion I called her after a lunatic ancestor— Leonora Cadiz. Only one of our ancestors was sane: he owned a bicycle shop in Hackney and no-one has ever been named after him.

Like her dead fathers, she matured faster than a responsibility. I weaned her on my peaches, waiting for the first hair to sprout from her loins. I fed the bodies of Wormy and Subaqua to Gilles de Rais, impaled on my trident and thrust through the bars of his cage. The former was a glove puppet without a hand; the latter was akin to a reluctant welcome.

I prepared the inside of the hall clock with soft cushions and vases of aphrodisiac flowers. Somewhere inside me, Sappho was stirring, clitoris ajar, waiting to strike sparks from the rub of flinty nipples, to loose a wine-dark effluvium from pulsating wounds.

When it happened, I bore Leonora over the temporal threshold, amid the boisterous cheering of Delves and mother. At long last, I enjoyed a true sexual release; we started at dawn and finished at dusk. I sounded each hour with a matching number of orgasms. Thus my pleasure waxed and waned like Sappho's breasts, which distilled and decanted lesbian milk. Delves and mother fought over the use of a wormhole, studying our lusts through the spokes of my multiple caresses.

I announced my pregnancy a week later. Having no more use for her, we locked Leonora in the attic. I rescued my pater's unearthed bones and nailed them into a low table. "A footstool carved from a single father!" I joked, while my stomach expanded.

With the aid of a stethoscope, I was able to listen to my own abdomen. I never heard the foetus kicking, but it often held forth on ethics. When my waters broke, I was relieved that the liquid was olive oil. The Reverend assisted at the birth; I screamed once as the child was plucked from my womb. There was no umbilical cord and the infant already possessed a beard.

We swaddled it in a toga and I fed it at my best nipple. Now it has grown into a mature philosopher and the world is more settled. This does not mean that we are at peace; far from it. But the oppressive weight of God has been lifted from our brains. Housewives float; they are grateful for this.

It is possible that our Plato's wisdom will decompose into the tongue of an Aristotle; but worries form the breakfast of life—similes have also become buoyant. At any rate, the reality of friendship finally exists, euphoric but not excessive. I know what it feels like: it is the passion of twins who share a single set of clothes. It is the narcissism of a self-abuser without hands.

About the Author

Rhys Hughes was born in 1966. His first book, *Worming the Harpy*, was published in 1995, and since that time he has published more than thirty other books and been translated into ten languages. His fiction is generally fantastical and his main influences are Italo Calvino, Boris Vian, Flann O'Brien, Donald Barthelme and Stanislaw Lem. His most recent book is the collection *Brutal Pantomimes* and he is now at work on an OuLiPo novel called *Comfy Rascals*. Fantasy, humour, satire, tragedy and philosophy are combined in his work to create a distinctive style. He incorporates paradoxes as entertainingly as he can into the plots of his stories.

Boiled Americans by Matthew Allen Rose

Boiled Americans is a puzzle box in book form, inspired by the violence of living in urban America and exploding the tendency to forget or ignore.

Great American Slasher by David C. Hayes

Baseball, apple pie . . . and murder.

The Bohemian Guide to Monogamy by Andrew Armacost

Here, a strange labyrinth of interlinked short fiction assembles itself into a darkly moving novella that deftly explores the bottomless pain and pleasure of love and commitment, the hinterland between youth and adulthood.

Surreal Worlds edited by Sean Leonard

An anthology of surrealistic compositions created by some of the finest names in genre fiction. A showcase of international talent undaunted by the conventions of language and common narrative structures. Here is timelessness. Here is Surreal Worlds

How to Succesfully Kidnap Strangers by Max Booth III

Do not respond to bad reviews. If you must respond to bad reviews, please do not kidnap the reviewer.

ADHD Vampire by Matthew Vaughn

He came, he conquered, he was distracted a lot

Notes from the Guts of a Hippo by Grant Wamack

A rugged journalist travels to Brazil in search of a missing hippo researcher and the notes left behind lead to something earth shatteringly revelatory.

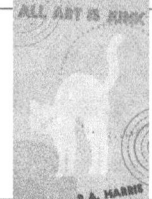

All Art is Junk by R. A. Harris

Lana Rivers, a girl with paintbrush hair, is missing and it's up to Lancelot, her cyborg knight, and his bionic conjoined twin, Cilia, to find her before her evil father, a disrespected artist turned mad-scientist, performs a terrible experiment on her.

Cherub by David C. Hayes

Cherub wasn't like the other boys—too slow, too rough—but he didn't deserve what that hospital did to him, and now he will make them pay.

Skinners by Adam Millard

Los Angeles, the City of Angels. At least, that's what the brochure says. What it fails to mention is the earthquakes. Oh, and the flesh-eating creatures lying dormant beneath the concrete, waiting for the chance to surface once again. Their wait is over . . .

The After-Life Story of Pork Knuckles Malone by MP Johnson

What's a farm boy to do when his pet pig becomes an evil, decaying hunk of ham with slime-spewing psychic powers?

A Lightbulb's Lament by Grant Wamack

A gentleman with a lightbulb for head wakes up in a world full of darkness, hooks up with a beautiful ex-prostitute, and an old man who can heal people; he travels down south to find the mysterious Creator.

The Horror Show by Vincenzo Bilof

A poetry novel—a narcoleptic, amnesiac Nobel Prize-winning poet becomes the subject of an experiment to cure madness.

Beyond by Jordan Krall

From Jerusalem to Mars, psychiatry and the unraveling of the universe

Gravity Comics Massacre
by Vincenzo Bilof

An absolutely shitty novella involving comic books, aliens, a serial killer, teenagers in an abandoned town, horror-trope dream sequences, and an ending you're going to hate.

Glue by Scott Lange

Sticky bowels and sticky situations.

Ascent by Matthew Bialer

Is the 8 foot tall creature haunting a small town in Iowa in the fall of the year 1903 the product of a hoax and collective imagination or was it one of the first documented paranormal event in America? This epic poem grapples with these questions.

Fecal Terror by David Bernstein

A killer turd is on the loose!

The Fairy Princess of Trains
by Christopher Boyle

Danny's mediocre life turns upside-down when his couch starts whispering to him. Then he's charged with a supernatural mission: Rescue the Fairy Princess of Trains.

Terence, Mephisto & Viscera Eyes
by Chris Kelso

9 new science fiction stories from Chris Kelso

Industrial Carpet Drag by Bruce Taylor

Chemicals make you do great things!

Bizarro Bizarro: An Anthology

The finest bizarro short stories from 2013.

Necrosaurus Rex by Nicolas Day

Necrosaurus Rex tells the tale of Martin, a simple janitor, who takes an unfortunate trip through time, becomes a violent mutant, and the father of us all. There's 14 billion years crushed inside these pages, and most of them are pretty nasty.

Day of the Milkman by S. T. Cartledge

In a world dominated by the milk industry, only one milkman survives after a terrible storm sinks all the ships and throws the Great White Sea out of balance.

Moosejaw Frontier by Chris Kelso

An unapologetic disaster of metafiction

The Boy Who Loved Death by Hal Duncan

From blackest humour to bleakest horror, with twisted relish, Hal Duncan's eighteen tales dig into death—and the life that goes with it.

www.ingramcontent.com/pod-product-compliance
Lightning Source LLC
Chambersburg PA
CBHW072031170626
46811CB00008B/3032